One Spark

"Imagination Begins with You…" 2020

Various Authors

One Spark

"Imagination Begins with You..." 2020

Compiled by Brian Claspell

Library of Congress Control Number: 2020940635

Cover design by Jasmine Mumford

Interior design by Jasmine Mumford and Brian Claspell

ISBN: 978-1-947315-06-8

ACKNOWLEDGMENTS

Many people have helped judge and make this high school writing contest possible. The stories are great.

I LOVE IT!

Thanks to all of the judges. Thanks to all of the teachers and administrators who encourage their students to participate. Thanks to all of the students who send in the stories. Thanks to my family who let me take a few weekends to judge. Thanks to my wife who prepares the awards and supports me in so many other ways.

2020 Winners and Finalists

Winner:

Escape! Feat. Floss   by Natalie Daines

Second Place:

The Hidden Colors of Mrs. John Holton   by Kate Voltz

Honorable Mentions:

Two Color Feathers   by McKinley Shoulders
Everything I Imagined   by Lauryn Taylor
A Hound and His Master   by Everette Brousseau
Conviction of Mind   by Naturi Scott
And She Smiled   by Emily Seaver
Copper Penny   by Dakota Kirk
A Good Day   by Sowmya Bulusu
She is a Writer   by Mary Ann M. Pangabiban
Good as New   by Jenna McFadden
Forever   by Alyssa Noseworthy

Finalists:

Stuck	Cleo Velvet Gifford Wear	They Are Wrong	Jordan Oldenburg
Tempered Glass	Keara Blankenship	You Don't Have to Understand	Ariana Dyer
Chat About It	Katharine Rottach	False Reality	Reagan Phelps
Leaving My Birthplace	Habiba Khatun	How I failed Algebra 2	Lisset
Do You Believe in Love at First Sight?	Blake Willett	Just Like Mama (2018 contest story)	Brianna
Chasing Heaven	Alicia Morelos	The Sparks That Ignite Us	Eliana Hansen
Organ Failure	Ariel S Levav	The Conversation That Changed Everything	Brooke Fertig
Caught	Ellie Sanders	Watch Out	Leanne Abel
The Goldsworth Problem	Elise Flor	How shopping malls came to be	Kate Sunshine
Grandfather Clock	Edison Luttrell	Sunflowers	Alyssa Smith
The Long Walk	Emmalyse Mason	With Wings as Eagles	Brenna Cothran
The Casanova	Jasmine Redo	Riverdale Bridge	Cody Bowen
Faded Lines	Gabriel Jenkins		

CONTENTS

Various Authors

SECTION 1 - MISUNDERSTOOD

Escape! feat. Floss

By Natalie Daines (2020 Winner)

"Bite the bullet, Oaklynn. Get it over with!" Mom said.

"If I do that, Mom, I won't be able to ever bite again. Who knows? Maybe I'll even die."

"We're here!" Mom chirped. "Hurry up!"

"But Mom, don't you love me? You're sending me to my death."

"Come on, honey, this isn't the time to fight."

I brightened up: "Will there be a right time later on?" She glared at me.

Dragging my feet through the door, I was greeted by a wrinkly, old woman. She smiled, but that didn't fool me. "Are you ready for your appointment, dear?"

"Nope," I turned to leave. Mom grabbed my shoulders and marched me to a chair.

"Come on, Oaklynn. If you don't get your cavity filled, it'll get worse."

Well, I was officially on my own. I scanned the waiting room, and started plotting my heroic battle and epic escape.

My eyes wandered over to the bowl of stickers on the counter. Stickers! I had a brilliant idea.

"Oaklynn Summers," a voice rang out.

Oh no. I wasn't ready yet. Panicking, I grabbed my chair and curled up like a toddler. Heroic? No. Effective? Maybe. Chuckling, the dental hygienist came to my side. "That's you, honey. You're our final patient for the day. Just take some deep breaths and follow me; we'll have you back here in no time."

My Mom joined in: "Oaklynn Mae Summers, get up right now or you won't have dessert for a month." Ouch. My Mom and the dental hygienist left the waiting room and went deeper into the dentist's lair.

I turned around and headed for the parking lot. My battle had not been epic, but I figured that if I walked fast, I could be in my tree house in half an hour. Unfortunately, Dr. Trout, the dentist, caught up to me. "Oaklynn, try to be reasonable. If we don't fill that tooth now, you're going to be in a lot of pain later on, and blah yadda ya blah blah..." My Mom came over and steered me back toward my doom.

I slipped free of my Mom and dashed to the sticker bowl, grabbing dozens of princesses, fluffy animals, and superheroes. Stunned by my weird behavior, all three adults stopped dead in their tracks and watched as I peeled the stickers. I jumped on a chair and slapped princess stickers over my Mom's eyes. "This has gone far enough!" my Mom thundered. Before anyone could do anything, I did the same to the hygienist and the dentist and ran for the door. Glancing back, I giggled at the commotion that filled the hallway.

Grabbing the doorknob, disaster struck. How could I have forgotten the wrinkly old receptionist? "Missy! You aren't getting away on my watch. Not if I can help it." Sputtering, I cried, "Oh yeah! Well, you... you... I'm sorry. You know, I'm not normally like this. I just, well, you know."

"Yeah, we know," Dr. Trout sighed. I was trapped. The receptionist blocked the door and the three others surrounded me. But I wasn't done fighting. Sometimes you have to give a little up to win, and I had a plan. "You know," I said in my most exhausted voice, "maybe we ought to call it a day." The hygienist disagreed, "We still have time. If you'll just come on back--"

I ran back to the procedure area, and climbed onto the counter. To the horror of all the adults, I climbed on top of the cabinet -- the ultimate place of refuge! My Mom yelped: "Oaklynn, you are eight years old. Stop acting like a baby."

I smiled. "Not until you promise to let me go home right now and never ever see a dentist again." All three adults blabbered on like earlier about the importance of maintaining good dental health. I started rummaging through a box of toothbrushes and floss that was next to me on the cabinet. One of the floss labels read: "Strong floss. Won't break."

"That's perfect!" I shouted. "So you'll come down, then?" pleaded Dr. Trout.

"Just a second!" Quickly, I ripped open a new toothbrush and floss onto it. I hurled the toothbrush around the swinging arm of the dentist's adjustable light like a grappling hook.

"Look out below!" I jumped off that cabinet like a great explorer. As I sailed through the air, clinging to my floss, visions of heroism and victory filled my head. Mom screamed, the hygienist fainted, and Dr. Trout stood there stunned.

Freedom was amazing. It was also short-lived. Crack! The toothbrush snapped in half. Smack! My two front teeth chipped after I landed face first on the polished, grey floor tile. Ironically, the floss didn't break. It really was that strong!

Waiting in the hospital to be checked out for concussion, I overheard Mom talking to Dad on her cellphone, "We'll go back tomorrow so Dr. Trout can fix Oaklynn's chipped teeth and fill her cavity. Can you take some time off to come to the appointment with me?"

I wasn't too worried. I had a plan. Before I left the dentist's office, I had grabbed the bits of my broken teeth and shoved them in a pocket. I know where Dad keeps the superglue at home. I can fix my own teeth. No problem.

Two Color Feathers

By McKinley Shoulders (Finalist and Honorable Mention)

Owl picked up the pace; he didn't want to miss the awakening of the world with its gentle colors. This autumn night had never been so cold. The crickets he never failed to hear were dull compared to his mother's stern voice echoing through his memories.

Owl had been in such a deep thought that he had missed his favorite part of the sun rising by the time he had scaled up the tree. The disappointment didn't faze him as he went back to the village. The walk would provide him opportunities to gaze at plants he missed on the trip there.

Owl was surrounded by the village children with the exception of Kai. Kai whose high rank could be seen by the swirls of dried blue paint he wore proudly on his chest and back. The runes of blue crept up his face and ended at his cheekbones. The same blue paint that Owl remembered his mother used to fuss over, "Owl the blue paint is not for you, not yet. Come help me so that your father can be seen by the tribe."

Owl jolted when the past faded and now Kai's stern face was glaring at him with disgust. Surrounding them were the village children eagerly watching. It didn't seem to matter that Owl had been on time from his early journey to attend Kai's afternoon lesson.

"Uncle-Chief Kai, on my journey nature has gifted me, so that I can heal mother." His small hands held out the precious berries he had spotted on his way back to the tribe.

"Berries?" Kai snatched the berries to examine and began to pace among the quiet children. "Can anyone tell me what property these berries provide?"

"Chief, They provide healing." The young girl known as Toma answered hesitantly.

Nagamao, another girl from the tribe, stood closely to Owl and whispered, "Owl, are you sure? The berries often look close..."

"Nagmao! This lesson is for Owl. Owl, take another look at these berries."

Owl leaned forth to do so; his eyes taking in the details of the berries. He frowned, there was nothing wrong with the berries he picked for his mother's health. "Wild blueberries Chief Kai."

"Tutsan." he accused.

Nagamao interrupted him, "Owl has been gifted with sight. Surely he'd be able to see the differences between the wild berries and Tutsan."

"These berries are Tutsan. Owl, I'm disappointed you could have harmed your mother."

Nagamao pressed further, "And Chef Kai, you've only looked at them once. Who's to say they aren't wild berries? You have not asked for a second opinion. You see only one way and Owl's eyes have the perspective of two men."

"Owl, take these poison berries and get rid of them! These berries are enough for the whole village."

Owl felt like he had a responsibility to set things right. The tribe's children had seen the wildberries in Kai's hand- what if the look and shape of the berries were ingrained in their minds? Owl knew with certainty the children could only see as much detail as Chief Kai; therefore, the slight color variation escaped their notice. This meant it was young Owl's responsibility to be the tribe's eyes for them.

"Owl and the rest of you, follow me!" Kai commanded.

There in the forest was a green bush wearing tutsan berries.

"Here are Wildberries." Kai declared. "We can tell by their shape and size."

"Chief Kai, the color-"

"Will tell you nothing!"

Toma tilted her head, "It's true wild berries and tustan appear to be the same color." She paused, her eyes adjusting to peer at Owl face, more specifically his eyes. "However, Chief Kai maybe Owl can see the color with his unique eyes. After all Nagamao mentions Owl has the sight of two men."

"Enough of this! I am your respected elder and chief. No one should question my authority. You think Owl wise, but Owl isn't so wise!" Kai shouted, anger now evident. With those short tempered words, Kai plucked the berries from the bush and swallowed them.

"I'm fine." Kai coughed.

Owl looked suspiciously at Kai on the walk back to the tribe with the day's lesson over.

In the whispers of the cool night Owl felt the touch of his mother's callous hands tapping his cheek. He woke. His mother's face was wet with tears. "Owl, you must flee this village!"

Owl didn't waste his time as he packed his things together, grabbing his water skin and the buffalo pelts. He turned to face his mother, who calmly sat at the end of their blanket. "Mother, are you not packing?"

His question went unanswered, and Owl knew he would have to leave alone. Had the village finally convinced his own mother he was a curse to the tribe?

"Owl, Uncle Kai is dead. I fear they will blame you. Remember you have everything to live for."

His mother pulled him in for a hug, and he realized it was the last time they would see each other.

He headed out of the tent without a backward glance

and was spooked when he recognized the outline of a human in the dark. Owl knew who it was. Nagamao. "Owl, I overheard you and your mother. Please before you leave take this with you." He held out his hand. She whispered, "They reminded me of your eyes."

He couldn't speak and didn't dare look at what she had given him as he rushed away disappearing further in the woods.

"You have everything to live for."

When Owl couldn't feel his legs, he sank in the soil, and his grief caught up with him. He opened his hand and revealed the gift. It was two feathers. One was brown and the other feather blue. He spoke to the owl he found watching him, "And what do I have to live for?"

He swore he could hear the owl answering back. Somehow the owl sounded like his mother.

"You."

Caught

By Ellie Sanders (Finalist)

I'm fine.

Two syllables, six letters, infinite meanings.

The boy couldn't remember the first time he'd heard that phrase. If he could've caught them, the words, in a clear, glass jar, he would've. First, he would've admired each individual letter, the smooth round top of the "f," the curious humps of the "m," the captivating curve of the "e," and finally, the knife-like point of the "i." He would've puffed out his cheeks and watched with intense fascination that only a child could have, gazing as the luminescent words glittered dangerously. He would've dissected them like they lived and breathed a life of their own, trying to affix a single meaning to their back, so that when he encountered them again, he could greet them as old friends. And finally, when all was said and done, he would've placed the jar in one of the gaping holes in his library of found words. And his mind would be at peace.

He reasoned that if he could've arrested the words when they'd first arrived, the poison that they'd spread in his life would've never existed. Yet every time he got out his net, they evaded him, always floating out of reach. He glanced down at his phone, at the glassy blue bubbles floating on the screen. The girl he'd held hands with on the way home had sent him one. This beautiful bubble had floated into his life one day and it'd been around ever since. He glared at his screen, hoping his gaze would force another one to appear. That another bubble would venture from the girl all the way to his screen and hover right next to his ear. It would pop softly and whisper that it was alright and she was ok. The boy blinked in surprise because it had, in fact, worked. As the small blue bubble made its tardy appearance, the boy squinted and frowned at it. The bubble, though disappointingly petite, was beautiful to the boy nonetheless. The phrase within the bubble, like a piece of glass, wore a disguise that beguiled and glittered. Yet when the boy reached to pick up the words, they cut him deeply, leaving their message inked on his skin. "I'm fine."

The boy was stunned at the dismissal, his chest constricting as his heart seized. His precious jars of words rattled and slid on their shelves as his cognitive cogs shuddered, trying to comprehend. Pain clouded the boy's mind and his stomach churned.

Over the years, the boy collected scars as he'd once collected words. As his collection amassed, he became more sensitive, more observant. The words took to following him, taunting him and making their presence known when the boy got too comfortable. They were there when his sister's heart shattered, his dad lost his job, and his mother filed for a divorce. The boy became acquainted with new words, sisters and brothers of the same breed and just as elusive. The boy met "I'm sorry" in the hospital room with his mother and "It's going to be ok" when his father appeared two hours later. The boy realized the more people he let in, the more the hurt inflicted by those words would continue to weigh on him. He was stumbling under the pressure and he felt the need to vomit- so he did. Agony raced through his body, causing his jars to shatter and his words to burst until it was all an incoherent jumble. Out of the depths of his heart and mind came the stream of fractured words leaking down into the recesses of his mind, taking the pain with it. Their sudden absence left the boy numb and winded. His shelves stood empty, but his mind was quiet.

Years later, outside the bookstore on North Hampton St., a man stood staring through the illuminated window. His body was full to the brim with words, so full in fact that he'd had to write many of them down so they wouldn't be forgotten. He blinked slowly, admiring how the lighting inside hit the featured book, his words, just so. His mind raced as he scoured his mental library for words that could express the emotions he felt. As he rummaged through his jars, he reflected on his life. Vast was his collection of jars, endless shelves of words and attached clouds of emotion. Although his collection was almost complete, no word felt right. Suddenly, through his haze of thoughts came a loud crash. Inside the store, a young woman had knocked over a book stand, books falling to the ground, pages sprawled open, stark black letters decorating cream paper. The man rushed into the store and approached the woman crouching on the ground inspecting the fallen soldiers.

He hesitated before asking tentatively, "Are you alright?"

She looked up in surprise, her lips spreading into a cheerful grin. She glanced at the mess and blushed before laughing softly and shaking her head at her own clumsiness.

"Thanks for asking," she said, shyly fiddling with the book in her hands. "I'm fine."

The man's mind balked at the words. The phrase, once sugar-coated, left a bitter reminisce. He peered at the woman, building up his walls as he tried to discern friend from foe. The woman met his gaze, sensing his uncertainty, the undercurrent of hurt.

"Truly," she said softly, "I'm fine."

The man's eyes widened, his mind and heart wary as he greeted the words again, like the old friends he'd once hoped they'd become.

"Come on," the woman laughed and grabbed his hand, pulling him towards the jumble of words and pages. "Help me clean up and I'll buy you coffee."

The man grinned back, his mind snaring her words and his heart capturing her smile, as they stooped down together and began collecting the words. The man peeked at her shyly, adding her image to his now finished collection, right next to the glittering, luminescent words, "I'm fine." And his mind found peace.

Everything I Imagined

By Lauryn Taylor (Finalist and Honorable Mention)

I laughed softly. My face was worn with lines indicating years of stress and tension. My smile indicated that it had all been worth it. I watched my daughter twirl around our small living room. Her brown eyes framed with long lashes and thick eyebrows shined as she spoke. "And look Mommy, there she is now." She leaned in, pressing her soft features onto the cold glass window. Her small fingers pointed towards a fluffy cloud in the distance. I smiled, "Yes honey, I see it too."

Of course, I knew nothing of the stories my young daughter told. I never quite saw the figures in the clouds or the sparkle showers from the sun that shone through the window. I didn't understand the detailed descriptions my daughter produced from short glimpses of strangers. To me, everything was the same. Clouds were clouds, sunlight was sunlight, and strangers were strangers. I loved her stories regardless. It reminded me of my once vivid but childlike imagination. Her mind was flexible and new. To her, the clouds were her friends and our living room was her stage. My daughter grew and with it her imagination. The stories created in her youth turned into beautiful paintings that scattered across the walls of the house. Her gentle paint strokes could be found on every available wall space. Light blue stripes in the living room, lively yellow dots in the bedroom, and green floral designs etched onto kitchen walls. I was always driving her to a new museum or taking her to drop off a painting at a local contest.

One afternoon, I found my daughter painting on a fresh canvas. Two shapes with matching chocolate tones appeared. "Who are they?" I asked. "It's us Mom," she replied. The painting showed two strikingly similar women standing in front of a mural on a beautiful building. The white columns framing the creation were chiseled and carefully detailed. The oldest woman beamed brightly at the younger woman. "This will be us Mom," my daughter softly spoke.

And in that instant, I woke up. I felt a bit dazed but an overwhelming feeling of joy erased all feelings of dizziness and doubt. The plain hospital room featured a painting mixed with blue lines, yellow dots and a green flower. I smiled. There was a gentle knock at the door. The nurse handed me a tiny face wrapped tightly in a hospital issued blanket. The chocolate skin paired well with my daughter's brown eyes. Our resemblance was undeniable. After all the struggle, I finally had my dream. "Congratulations Ms. Ray," the nurse smiled brightly. I imagined how much my life had changed and how much it would change. All this had started with me. I hoped my daughter would have everything I imagined.

The Long Walk

By Emmalyse Mason (Finalist)

The night was frigid. The feeling of guilt tickling at my throat as I kept trudging through the snow. I had left my only friend to die within this valley, and I could not handle the tsunami of what was yet to come. With the fire burning out, I had decided to take our only oxen left, and loaded what was left of our supplies onto its broad and sturdy back. But there was no taking back my actions. If one of us were to survive, it had to be me. I was going to make it to Oregon. With or without him. The devils danced about me, whispering crimes and vicious noises in my ear. "How lovely" they sneered, "you bide by the devil's rules now girl." I swatted behind me as if the apparitions would be affected by my physical form. But alas, it was only me and my oxen, both heads clattering their horns together, nothing but the wind giving us life in this barren crevice.

Faded Lines

By Gabriel Jenkins (Finalist)

Two extraordinarily pale kids, a boy and girl of seventeen, found a place to sit behind the school during their lunch period. It was the middle of March and they had not seen the sun in over three months. But it was back today and the spot they picked was strategic, drenched in light. They sat in silence, for what they did was a focused task. Sleeves were rolled up and socks were rolled down. Surface area was the object of their game. Side by side, they soaked sunlight into their skin like anthropomorphic sponges. They closed their eyes, tilted their chins up, and smiled. The light fed them. It gave them summer energy. It penetrated their eyelids, glowing them red with translucence and illuminating tiny rivers of veins that flowed across. The cartilage at the edge of their ears shone brilliantly. They could feel their blood moving. Winter was finally gone and their bodies had come alive.

Dory was the girl's name. Her boyfriend was Rory. This ritual was rare, as the sun seldom showed itself, but they participated whenever they could. The two kids had dangerously pathetic vitamin D levels. Their blood didn't have enough calcium in it. So on days like today they would sit and absorb as much of the sun's life-giving rays as they possibly could. The sun's magic was intoxicating. Back in class, Dory rubbed her eyes to dispel the lingering brightness of morning. Her legs jittered, bobbing up and down and twitching above the floor. Being kept inside today was injustice. It took all of her willpower not to run back out.

Dory hated her teachers and her classmates. Learning was best done outside in the world, she thought. In the dark classroom, she stared at the chalkboard and all its faded lines. She studied them intently. All their curves, their starts, their ends. It was her little game. Dory would pick the start of a line to trace with her eyes, and if she was lucky, be able to follow it all the way to its end point. Dory usually got lost in the middle of the board, which was a dangerously ambiguous white cloud. She both loved and despised the day when the janitor came in after hours to wipe the board down with chemicals. Her game was easier for a while, but she had to start over with brand new players.

When she tired of the lines, she put her head between her arms. Classroom noises provided a steady drone to lull her into serenity. Sometimes they would inspire sleep and sometimes they would inspire dreams. Today she dreamt a memory. It was a soccer practice of her freshman year, the year before she had to quit. At some point during each practice in October, the players froze in their place to stare west. Above the highway and rush hour traffic, the sun slowly shrunk behind the mountains, dyeing the surrounding sky shades of heaven. Everyone on the field was held captive by the sight. Dory saw

God up there. Eventually though, the horizon swallowed up the sky and darkness came. She closed her eyes and held on for just a little longer than everyone else, though. On her eyelids remained a canvas of beauty.

She woke up. Something the teacher said must have snapped her into consciousness. She looked up at him. He was scraping a message across the board with his pearly stub. Dory wondered how much of that precious mineral was being scraped away for her education. He tossed the stub down on his desk. All that calcium wasted. He swiped across the board violently with a black cloth. What a tragedy, she thought, to sacrifice her body for her mind. The chalk evaporated into powder dust, then floated towards an open window. Dory knew it was stupid. She did. But she held out her tongue. She closed her eyes, imagining how the lovely, disgusting, nourishing dust would taste. She thought it might taste like sunlight, like soccer practice, like sitting outside with Rory. When she opened them, she found herself back in the dark classroom looking at the board. Dory had another faded line to study. And she couldn't find the end of this one.

They Are Wrong

By Jordan Oldenburg (Finalist)

They say sirens are instruments of death. That the gods themselves made us to punish those who do not abide by their rules and traditions. They are wrong.

The sea created us. She took pity on us, remade us into what we are now from the brink of death. The murders of my sisters and I were unjust; brought on by the suspicion and hatred of foolish mortal men who searched for anything to blame their misfortune on. Women just so happened to be convenient.

So they stripped us, tied our legs together with heavy ropes and dragged us by our hair to the edge of the ship. They spat on us, cursed us, and then threw us into the water with hardly a thought. They left us to die.

And slowly, as the frigid water crept into our lungs and we sank below the once-beautiful rays of moonlight, something changed us. A gentle presence relieved us of the pressure on our chests. Turned the water from what was choking us and into something we gasped for like it was air. Our legs, bound together and made immobile by the ropes, began to fuse together.

My sisters tell me of identical memories.

When it was over, and my body shuddered with the memory of pain and fear and something I still cannot place, a soothing voice surrounded me.

You are safe now, daughter. Your name is Ceto, and you will have your revenge.

I struggled to the surface, despite the fact that I no longer struggled to see in the dark waters. When I finally breached the surface, I took in a hesitant breath and found that I could breathe air as well as water. My eyes picked out a tiny speck on the dark horizon, and a snarl escaped me as I realized what it was.

The men who had tried to kill me were on that ship. And I would return the favor, even if it killed me. So I dove beneath the water and raced the current. When I caught up, a crack of thunder reached my ears even below the surface, and lightning illuminated the world for a split second. The captain shouted to drop anchor for the storm, and a smile nearly crossed my face.

I do not know how. But when I broke the surface and opened my mouth, a melody poured out. Words I'd never uttered before, with a voice that had never sounded so sweet.

Do not fear the raging water, my love

For it is much nicer here than above

Join me here, beneath the waves

Join me, dear, now just be brave

The words continued coming, as I spoke of their deepest desires and darkest secrets. They drifted to the edge of the boat as if in a trance, all of them with blank smiles on their face and eyes peering at nothing. I continued.

I know what it is you fear

What you wish for most is clear

If you listen to the words I speak

I will help you find the truth you seek

And they jumped. One by one until all four of them were in the water and their ship was left empty. As I approached them, their gazes grew dreamy, and I smiled at them. "You do not need to swim. Just relax. Look at me, look at the sky. Do not worry about staying afloat." So they did not. They stopped swimming, and I watched with the same smile until they were so deep that not even I could make them out.

It has been centuries since that night. Every memory besides that one of my former life is gone. Faded into blurred faces and wondering if I did something good with my life before then. I am not good anymore.

Tonight my sisters and I join to wait for our next meal. A mighty storm brews, and the only sound is the crash of water against water and the hull of the ship. This ship is big, sleek and shiny with a deck taken up by what must be twenty humans.

They shout in a language we have long forgotten, words slurred by the drinks they consume and toss cups of overboard. Soon, once the storm breaks, we will rise to the surface. The magic in our blood will supply us with words we do not know and the knowledge of what our victims wish for most. It is with this that we lure them.

Alone, one of us can lure a few people; more if they are like-minded. Together, my sisters and I can take down ships far bigger than this one. We have before, and we will again.

And then, a boom of thunder reaches even our ears. I can't help but smile. We swim to the surface, breaking out of the water almost simultaneously.

They say that within every siren is a human girl, begging to be free and crying with each life that is taken.

They are wrong.

Just Like Mama

By Brianna (2018 Finalist and Honorable Mention)

Ever since I was a little girl, I knew I wanted to be just like Mama. After all, I was named "Julia Grace" after my Mama's mother. When I was three, I copied everything she did. But she never seemed to mind. I sat with her during church on Sundays. When she would cross her right leg over her left, I would too. When she reached for the book of hymns, so did I. Then I opened up to the page, and was disappointed that I could not read yet. Somehow magically sensing my frustration, my mother would lean over and whisper the words in my ear so I could sing with her. When I was five, I noticed how Mama was always cooking something up in the kitchen. I would tug on her skirt and say, "What are we making today, Mama?" She would tell me what we were having for dinner and place me on the counter. I wanted to cook just like Mama. So she would give me little jobs to do. I would crack eggs or mix biscuit dough. I didn't do it very well and Mama would always have to clean up my mess. But she was happy to do so. My Mama had the patience of a saint. By the time I was ten, Mama and I made cooking together a habit. Biscuits were our favorite thing to make and we made them perfect. We would make them every week on Sunday mornings before we went to church. When someone we knew got sick, Mama sent them some of our biscuits. Just like Mama, I started sending biscuits to my sick friends too.

Eventually, my childhood ended and it was time for me to leave Mama's home. I called Mama everyday while I was in college, and I came home to visit almost every weekend. I would tell her about my week as we made some biscuits. She would always send me back to college with more than half of them, even when we made enough to feed an army. "College students are always sick of something," she claimed. "Sick of school, sick of drama, sick of being away from their Mamas." She winked at me. "So you'll need them sooner or later." She was always right about that. The biscuits reminded me of home. They always got me through a bad day. I met a boy at college and I married him in the same wedding dress Mama wore to her wedding. Mama brought me biscuits when I had my first baby, and my second, and my third. Life couldn't be any better. I went through a checklist in my head. I learned to sit like Mama. Check. I learned to sing like Mama. Check. I learned to cook like Mama. Check. I learned to share like Mama. Check. I went to college like Mama. Check. I got married and had a few adorable children just like my Mama did. Check and check. I was well on my way to making Mama proud of me.

When I was only forty-eight years, Mama got sick, really sick. Forty-eight years knowing Mama wasn't enough. But the doctors were saying that was all I was going to get. I did what my Mama had done for everyone she knew when they were sick. I made some homemade biscuits and took them with me to the hospital. With my family all gathered in the small hospital room, we knew it was time to say goodbye to Mama. The minutes and hours ticked by as she visited with her children and grandchildren one by one. She shared her love and her wisdom with each one of them. "Julie Grace," she called in a hoarse voice. "May I speak with you?" I sat at her bedside as I tried to hold back my tears. "Don't you be afraid to cry now," she said gently patting my head. "Oh, Mama," I cried. "All I ever wanted was to make you proud." I handed her the biscuits I made, unable to say another word without sobbing. Mama smiled warmly. "You are my pride and my joy, Julie Grace. Don't you ever forget it!" Mama said this with such resolve that I couldn't help but smile. "Yes, ma'am." I replied. I gave her one last embrace and kissed my Mama on the forehead. The next time I saw Mama, she was sleeping peacefully in a casket. Before she was lowered into the ground, I placed a single pink carnation on her casket. "I love you, Mama." I whispered. I now live my life in preparation for the day I go to heaven. Just like Mama.

The Sparks That Ignite Us

By Eliana Hansen (Finalist)

I watched mesmerized as frost formed slowly on my fingers. The cold ate away at me and my bones felt frozen and brittle. The icy wind burned away at me, but if anything I had never felt more warm and safe in my entire life. Even as my knees shook and my toes sunk in the snow, I had never felt more at home. I closed my eyes and let the snow consume me.

When I was younger, I had always preferred the cold. It was comforting and numbing. My house had always felt hot, as if it was a furnace. Even in the dead of winter when we lost power, it was suffocatingly hot. I had always preferred to sit outside on the steps, my bare feet on the freezing concrete, testing how long I could hold it this time.

My father was the source of the heat. He radiated it. A fiery anger coursed through him. I never talked to my father, and he only yelled at me. I was a nuisance, a mistake, a psycho. I was nothing like him. Even though his words were loud, I never really heard him. My mother had told me it was the whiskey that set him on fire. However, I knew that all the whiskey did was fuel him. My father was never a nice man, and he had set himself on fire.

My mother told me that I was like her. She even made me shave my head like hers. My father called us freaks and monsters, my mother called us unique. I blame her more than my father. I could dodge a kick and ignore his heated words, but she was a broken shard of glass that lodged itself in me. I don't think I will ever be able to get it all out. I hope I never end up like her.

There was only one place for me to hide. It was cool and dark and it was mine. I could hear my father yelling, but the darkness kept me safe. The gravel under the house would scrape my arms and legs, but I kept crawling, trying to go deeper into the recesses. That was my space, in the darkness, anything could be true. I would squeeze my eyes shut and pretend to be far away, deep in a cave somewhere, the drip of water and the squeak of bats as my only companions. I imagined I was anywhere but home.

Sometimes when the yelling was loud enough to be heard even deep under the house, in my secret cave, I took to the woods behind our house. It was a sparse cluster of trees, but if I climbed a special tree high enough, I couldn't be seen from the house. That is where I kept my treasure. A decrepit birdhouse balanced precariously on a branch and inside, wrapped in a cloth, was my doll. The face was faded, and the original clothes were long gone, but her hair had been meticulously brushed and kept clean. I had also made her a dress, of sorts, from an old tee shirt I had outgrown. She was my pride and joy. She was my best friend, and my only friend.

Sometimes she was a fairy who could grant one wish, sometimes we were runaways or Indians, but mostly she was someone to talk to. I told that doll everything, and while I talked I would practice braiding her hair. She was a good listener. I told her what I wanted to do and who I wanted to be, and she listened. She was the only one I told of my plan, but she didn't see it executed.

The day I decided to leave, a heavy fog settled and a monotonous rain sputtered down. I took my doll, and my raincoat, ready to leave. I made it down the street, when I heard a child crying and ducked behind a trash can. I still picture that child, but she never saw me. She sat on the curb, her face bleeding and her arms and legs covered in bruises and cuts. Her pale blue dress was stained with dried blood and mud. Her hair was dripping wet. She couldn't have been more than seven.

Indistinct yelling from one of the homes made her jump to her feet, turning her back to me in search of the voice. She stood there long enough for me to place my doll nearby her on the pavement and return to my hiding spot. I didn't want to part with her, but that little girl needed her. I shoved my hands in my pockets, fidgeting with the lighter I had stolen from my mother. I was going to miss my doll and only companion, but the girl and my doll both had on the same color dress. Besides, I didn't need her anymore. I was getting out. That is all I can let myself remember, that was the day of my first and last smile. That is the day I have done nothing but try to forget since it happened.

I opened my eyes, not wanting to drift too far into the past. I shivered, but not from the cold. As my hand shook, the frost turned to freezing droplets and fell to the ground. I could feel the heat rise inside me, as I struggled to keep it down. Perhaps it was my imagination, but the falling snow sizzled when it hit my skin, steam rising off me. I grabbed at handfuls of snow trying to bury myself with the comforting numbness, but it all melted away. I could hear my parents calling out to me, my father screaming that I was nothing like him, and my mother singing sweetly. Instinctively I reached for my mother, hating myself even as she held me close. In her sing song mantra, she cooed softly, "Just like me, just unique. Can't have a fire without a spark. Just a little spark." She gripped my arms like iron, "You're just like him, just unique. Just a little spark, just a little spark." Her voice turned into a strangled shriek, "How could you, how could you?"

The smell of ashes suffocating, a heat pressed down on my chest. I could feel a needle in my arm and my body relaxed. The cold darkness swallowed me up again. I stood on a snowy mountain, watching as frost climbed up my arms and wind whipped against me. Even in that bitter cold, I had never felt more at home.

SECTION 2 – REGRETS

Conviction of Mind

By Naturi Scott (Finalist and Honorable Mention)

"Mom, I'm going out!" I yell up the stairs.

There's no reply. She never answers anymore. It's been like this for months now. My therapist says tragedy does that to people; It makes them create an alternate reality, living in a half-conscious stupor until their brain can catch up. It makes them forget, she says, about the ones here; in this case me.

Walking down the path, the cool air hits my face. The neighborhood is comfortably silent. Like the night before a storm, except the sky's clear and the worst is behind us now. Behind, though not far. Not far enough at least.

On days like today, I wish I couldn't think.

"Thoughts can be dangerous," my therapist whispers.

I know. I know. I KNOW. I KNOW THIS BETTER THAN ANYONE.

This silence is deafening. Why today? Why not on any other day? I can't walk fast enough. I wish I could clear my head. I need to clear my head.

"Hi."

The little boy's voice interrupts my absorption. I've never seen him before or at least I don't think I have. His slender form quivers against the breeze as he uses his twig-like arms to provide an inch of warmth. He's about 8 or 9, maybe older, either way, he's small for his age. His face is vaguely familiar, but then again I've seen many faces...Licking my lips, I turn to him.

"Hello."

"Mikey?" he chokes out.

"Uh...yeah. It's Michael though. How do you know my name?" Confusion lingers on the tip of my tongue. I've never seen this boy before. There's no way he could possibly know me. I bet it's this town. Everyone is always talking, gossiping. It's a pitiful cliché really. How disgusting. Disaster strikes someone else's life and all they can do is mock their suffering. It's incorrigible. Have they sent this boy to torment me?

"What do you want?" I add seething.

"Uhhh..." He doesn't finish, taking off down the street the way I came.

Good.

Discomfort abruptly rakes throughout my body. I feel a

twinge of remembrance. Yes, I remember now. I'm on a mission. That boy only set me back. He knew what he was doing all along. I knew it, too. But no distraction is powerful enough to deter me. I let purpose take me away. Far away. Further away than the depths of my mind can reach. I can feel my feet pounding, my breath waning, my heart pounding with excitement. The cold air fills my body. It enlivens me. Winter is my sanctuary.

Squinting my eyes open, everything is in pain. I can't make out much, but I know it's nighttime. The high moon above tells me that it is around 1 am. I can see my breath as it escapes me, rising in the dim moonlight, disappearing to cycle through another creature. Slowly rising from the ground, my bones creak in desperation. I don't know how long I've been out here, but I can feel dirt and grim in every pore of my skin. Just what am I doing out here?

Shaking my head, I try to scramble some thought together. As I fully examine my surroundings, I am horrified.

The gravestones stare into my soul. They know what I've done.

Turning around, I screech. What have I done?

Walking backward in disbelief, I feel something under my feet. A shovel.

Tears are now streaming down my face.

A grave in front of me is all dug up.

The sirens draw nearer.

What...How am I going to explain this?

Panic immobilizes me. Standing and Staring are the only functions of my body. The world is in a blur. I feel myself being tackled. I cannot prepare for the fall that's to come. They force me into a straight-jacket. How odd? Everything is baffling.

Yanking me to my feet, they drag me away. For a brief moment, my eyes glimpse the excavated graves' headstone. It too taunts me.

"In loving memory of Amelia Reye who will always be remembered by her sons..."

Organ Failure

By Ariel S Levav (Finalist)

Oh, I suppose it's time for my daily dose of Emmoron.

You're not supposed to feel the infusion, but I always try to.

It brings me back to reality.

I rose from a fetal position on the couch and planted my feet on the floor, curling my toes into the carpet. My overgrown toenails snagged the light brown fibers as I stretched, creating the uncomfortable sensation of cracking and pulling. I didn't mind, however, and ripped my feet from entanglement to walk to the opposite side of my apartment. The walls of my one-room were empty and blank, exposing the off-white color seen in most practical designs. The texture of the sturdy drywall was coarse and unpleasant, so I often avoided leaning on the walls. Most of the time I stood to the side of the room, near the door.

My armband clicked and I looked down at the screen embedded amongst the panels to see what it was doing. The assortment of flashing lights indicated my heart rate and the time, among other things. I could never be sure if it was the real time as there were no windows to see what was outside.

I watched the seconds of my life tick by, not thinking about their meaning; just occupying my ever decaying mind. Mindlessly staring at the life-controlling device, I stood in silence. The flashing display numbed my mind until I had forgotten what I was doing in the first place. Shuddering suddenly, I sat back down on the comfortable couch and glanced at the door.

After a moment, the door opened silently and my Keeper stood in the frame, not menacing but not friendly either. The Keepers were an interesting species; as far as I knew, they were purely mechanical. They moved with a frictionless grace, never making a mistaken turn in the seemingly endless halls and maze-like structure of the building. Their hard exterior was smooth, and the ovular design contained no straight lines; I guess it made it harder for people to grab on to it.

My Keeper moved back out of the doorway into the hall. I followed cautiously, as I did every time. When I was younger and naïve, I was full of curiosity and the need to explore. I asked questions, exclaimed with joy about simple things such as my newfound lack of hunger, and wandered aimlessly in the vast halls of the desolate complex. Eventually, I grew used to the technology and stopped caring. Then the Keepers were able to herd me with the rest. I became a mindless, emotionless, shell of a human; able to exist in my body but with very little connection to it. My brain, heart, stomach, and nerves were controlled by the device; it provided me with sustenance, health, and even feelings. It did all of my bodily functions for me at such a fast and unnoticeable pace that I could go days without realizing my body is there. I was untethered, just a human spirit in a fleshy, mechanical body.

After what seemed like an eternity of walking down the countless halls, my Keeper guided me into the work facility. It led me to a vacant spot in front of one of the monitors lining the rows of the cavernous room and sat me down. The reflectionless black screen flashed to life before my eyes, starting my day of work. I could sense the monotony setting in already, and I began to glance around at my fellow detainees. There was something inherently interesting about the lack of control of facial expressions that most people had. However, detached from their bodies they got, they still reacted on a physical level to mental stimulation.

One woman seemed different; as if she was truly living in the world instead of being able to block it out. My detachment allowed me to notice changes in other people much better than if I had to focus on my own body. This separation of mind and body was necessary to survive in this environment. Observing this woman, I got the sense that it was not something she possessed. Whenever I saw her, she appeared agitated and restless. Today, she looked nervous. She kept glancing around; not with the calm interest that I had, but with an aura of paranoia that was only growing stronger. She looked like she was afraid of being caught doing something she knew was wrong.

I stared at her for what must have been hours because

by the time she was picked up by her Keeper, I was also being disconnected and shepherded back to my room. I kept thinking about her, with what at one point, in my more human body, could be considered a passion, but now was dulled to a mere curiosity. I thought about her through the hours that I sat in the dark room, waiting for the next time I would see her at work.

I guess a day had passed because I once again noted the Emmoron infusion. My Keeper arrived at the same time as usual, and the routine walk ensued. I arrived at my workstation and got settled in, then began my visual hunt for the woman.

She didn't show.

All day, between my bored glances at the screen and scanning the room, I didn't see her. It was as if she had vanished. Never before had I noticed someone not being at work from one day to the next; only new people coming in.

I was guided back to my room and the routine repeated again. Still no sign of her.

Unsurprisingly, it only took me three work cycles to completely forget about the mysterious woman, and as the final thoughts of her slipped my mind, I wondered what else I may have forgotten during my time here. This facility, this life, was never what I wanted. I had been reduced to just another number in the system.

And I guess I'll have to be okay with that.

Stuck

By Cleo Velvet Gifford Wear (Finalist)

I didn't know where I was. Something felt different, as if a blinding fog had swallowed me whole. A sudden chill ran up my spine. It felt as if I was frozen. I couldn't see anything. I tried to move, but I couldn't. I was stuck. Stuck to what?

I looked down to what seemed like a normal wooden chair. I couldn't see the floor, or anything else for that matter. Everything was black, and dull, except for the chair. I tried to sit up, tried to leave the chairs hardwood arms, but no. I couldn't get up. I was trapped. There was something else, a scratch mark on the left side of the chair. It was as if a huge wolf had tried to attack it. But, unlike a wolf attack, there was only one mark, one perfect scar. I looked out into the distance, the fog still pressing against my very soul. I fought against the cold stinging fog. I pushed back my tears. I tried to run, tried to scream, tried to make my pain disappear. Then darkness. Nothing but darkness. I looked up, squinting. I saw something, a spec of color. The colors grew and grew until they came together to form the most beautiful garden I had ever seen. The garden was full of tropical flowers, and there was a stream flowing to what seemed like the end of the earth. I wanted nothing more than to touch that water. That cool crystal that could soothe my throat, soothe my pain. But, I was still stuck. I looked back down at the chair, which had revealed several more scars. Each mark represented a day that I was trapped here in this hell. I began to cry, the tears pouring down my frozen face, falling against nothing. Nothing at all. I was stuck. I spent my time looking at the stream, wishing that one day I could drink from it's humble arms.

It was just like any other day. My body had grown numb. It was as if I had become the chair. The garden was alive and well. I was sitting there, looking straight out into it's wilderness, when I heard it. A voice, soft at first, as if a song was playing inside of my head. It was a woman's voice, so familiar, so normal. I wasn't afraid of her voice. I was afraid of what she was saying.

"Come back to me," she sang as if her heart had been ripped out.

"Please I can't lose you," she was crying. Her tears stained my ears. I wanted it all to stop. I wanted her to go away. Go away! Go away! She never left. Every single moment was misery. I could hear her screams, crying every single passing moment. I wanted her to stop. She had to stop. Or I would go insane. I had to find her, tell her everything would be okay, beg her to stop screaming. I had to move. I had to run, follow her voice. But I was stuck to this chair. I had become paralyzed from the waist down. How could I possibly move? The chair was now completely covered in scars, the wooden splinters bleeding into my helpless body. I thought that the chair might break under my weight. It did break, it shattered into a thousands pieces, and I fell. I couldn't catch myself. I couldn't call for help. I was lying on my back in the fog. The garden vines were crawling against my skin. Their thorns were burning, and tearing at my hands, and my legs. My body lay bruised, and vulnerable. I was broken and shattered just like the chair. I was stuck in the darkness, stuck in the fog, stuck to the wooden corpse of the chair. The voice kept ringing in my ears louder and louder until I just couldn't take it any longer. I screamed. I screamed so loud I thought I would break. And then, a blinding light, silence. I squinted, looking up at the hospital lamp that had shined on my skin for so long. Next to me I saw my family crying, and signing some documents. No. No they couldn't. I'm here! I'm back! Don't make me go back! Don't make me stay there! But it was too late. They couldn't see me. Their grief blinded them. The sadness sucked the air out of my lungs, as the nurse unplugged me, sentencing me to nothing. To darkness. To sadness. I saw their tears as they left me cold, and lifeless in that hospital bed. They watched as every piece of life left my body, the warmth, the softness, the air. There was no air.

The moment they let me go, I was free. I went back to my shattered chair. I went back to the garden. I walked into the wilderness. I smelled every flower. I ran through every path. I stared into the crystal blue stream. I touched the cool water. The stream began to laugh, pulling me towards it, dragging me into the depths of its arms. I let it pull. I let it consume me. It swallowed me whole. Now, I'm stuck forever in its grasp, forever alone. My life is over. But yours isn't. Wake up. Please wake up.

Tempered Glass

By Keara Blankenship (Finalist)

I sat there, listening to the beat of my heart, realizing all that was a dream, I drew a breath of relief. I knew what they were doing in the Lab. Sending people into the abyss of Time Travel... taking their whole life and throwing it in the trash. I couldn't stand living 1 day in a glass orb, flying around in the world I've known for 18 years. My light shaggy brown hair lay across my shoulders as I stretch and get up from my bed. I mope over to the other end of my room and grab my leather red jacket. Heading out the door and down the stairs to the main living area, I stopped to say bye to Mom and Dad. I took the picture frame and softly kissed the picture with them from a few years ago inside, holding memories only my mind could reproduce. When I was younger, my parents took their life. Into orbs of glass. They found a way to communicate with each other, disobeying the rules and causing them to go into a traumatic seizure. Killing both of them, my aunt took me under her wing. I live with her now. "Bye Chrysal" I said walking by her as she knit her scarf out of elegant purple and baby blue yarn. She looked at me with a warm smile and turned back toward her project. I left our old worn out apartment and headed out.

Today I was going to go to give food to people in need. People left over from the Wipeout... I made my way down BlackWood Street and headed to the old abandoned hospital. Several people walked by me to the hospital with food, blankets, toys for the children. My attention slowly shifted from the people to the Labs, a large killing machine. I got side tracked and began heading South towards the Labs...

It was early Monday morning, and no one was anywhere. I thought there would be at least 3 or 4 cars or people walking but... nothing.I started to creep toward the gate that read KEEP OUT! The gate had already been opened and broken. I slipped through a hole in the gate and stood staring at the Lab. I looked to my left and saw nothing but an open, field full of dead, broken trees. They looked like someone came and sucked the life out of them. I walked over to a wilting tree and touched its trunk. The dark frail oak trickled down the trunk and hit the ground, shattering into tinnier pieces. It reminded of my thoughts of an Orb being dropped... Shattering into shards of glass and covering the floor in sparkles.

I phased out of my imagination and left for the Lab.

It took me about 20 minutes to reach the Lab. The door to the inside of the Lab was slightly cracked open but not enough to where I could pass through. I struggled to push the heavy iron weight door to get inside. I pushed and shoved and finally got in. It was dark and smelled of chemicals. There where glass orbs all over the ground, broken and shattered .I walked

46

carefully over the shattered orbs and got to a computer. The computer was on. Everyone died... how is ONE computer on and in PERFECTLY good shape? Maybe it was a Jumper trying to hack files... I sat down in the dust filled chair and tampered with the computer. There are A LOT of files about orbs. These people were maniacs about orbs. Then there was one file. ORB DISOBEY. I opened the file and tears filled my eyes. I read all the deaths that happened because they didn't follow the rules of ORBS. I scrolled through all the names while trying not to cause a lot of noise, thinking that there may have been a Jumper in the facility. Tears blurred my vision as I reached the end. I stared at the computer monitor and wanted to punch through its old dirty glass monitor. ENTRY 552626: 2 victims. Mother, 36 years. Father, 39 years. 1 daughter taken as Tortured. I pushed the chair away from the computer and tripped, falling into the corner, crying. Mom.... Dad.... I couldn't hold it back. It showed a picture of they're bodies after they had the seizure. Pale white, and wrinkly corpses. I wish they were still alive today. I wish I could just see them one last time before it happened. Just to hear my mother's sweet voice and smell my father's cologne. I'd do anything to have them back...

I heard something move in the room a few doors down. There was a dim light shining through the doorway. I started to walk toward the room and stopped as I heard a boy's voice. I figured it was a Jumper and ran back to grab a piece of an orb, sharp enough to stab.

It was Tyler.

Tyler was close to our family before the cleanse, and after they came... we lost each other. His parents died shortly after, and due to that, we were left as Tortured. Many kids were captured and tested, thus earning the name Tortured. They locked us up, tested us, laughed and beat us... and before they went completely psycho and killed off everyone, I escaped. I haven't stepped foot in that room since then. I was too afraid. Too afraid that I'd hear the screams of the other kids... Too afraid that by stepping in the light I'd see my old room... Every last scratch on that door. Every bloodstain on my bed..

I've been alone for some time, fending for myself... And now, my story begins with finding a way to destroy this... crystal nightmare I find myself in. This.. world filled with Tempered Glass.

The Goldsworth Problem

By Elise Flor (Finalist)

Tinsley ran his slender fingers across the starchy paper of the phone book scanning the pages for one name in particular: Goldsworth. The infamous family was wrapped up in yet another scandal of Titanic sized proportions and Detective C.C. Tinsley was determined to not let them get away with it again.

Elizabeth Short, known in the media as the Black Dahlia, was bisected and found two weeks ago on the fifteenth of January dumped in Leimert Park, Los Angeles. Most people in the general public believed that one Dr. George Hodel was her killer, because of his connections with the victim as well as prior allegations of this sort. This attracted attention from any reporter worth his salt in the Los Angeles county area. The only thing strange about that, other than the obvious murder, was that there were no actual statements from Dr. Hodel, always from one of the Goldsworths.

See, whenever the media would question him about it,

a member of the Goldsworth family or someone in their employ would swoop in and answer all of them, thus putting all doubts to bed. This was the highest profile murder case of the century, and no one was talking about it. The whole thing was fishy to say the least, and nothing was being done.

Tinsley slammed the last phone book shut in a huff as he failed yet again to locate any record of the name Goldsworth. Not a single person. He had tried looking for the family's allies and found nothing. He had been to every library in L.A. and found not a single word on any of them. How was that even possible, it was 1947 for Pete's sake? Tinsley himself had miles of articles published about him, and he was only a private detective who snooped in peoples' business.

Tinsley gave a pathetic attempt at a wave in the direction of the disgruntled librarian as he pushed his way out the front doors of the building. He began walking to his car, an unlit cigarette dangling loosely from his lips. Stopping to lean against the hood of his car, Tinsley lit up and took a long drag.

"What a lousy detective I am," he muttered to himself.

"On the contrary, sir," a stranger countered. "We just don't want you to find anything."

Tinsley stared wide-eyed at the man, he had come seemingly from nowhere. He wore a bespoke suit and stood in a way that made it look to passersby as if the two were old friends, when in fact they were not.

"If you would kindly follow me, there is someone who would like to meet with you," the man eluded, turning on his heel and walking in the opposite direction of where Tinsley intended to go.

Tinsley checked his surroundings before following, fully aware that following the man was quite possibly the stupidest thing he could have done. He should be getting is his car and driving as far away from this mysterious man as fast as possible, checking behind him at every traffic stop to make sure no one was following him. He shouldn't be following him into an alley. He shouldn't be moving towards the open car door that was offered to him. He shouldn't be sinking into the darkened back seat of a spotless '43 Cadillac.

"Detective Tinsley," a voice greeted from the seat next to him, the face connected to it shrouded in darkness. "I've heard you're looking for me and my family."

"Are you a Goldsworth?" Tinsley asked then internally chided himself, of course he was a Goldsworth.

"Yes," the voice confirmed with what sounded like a coy chuckle. "Ricardo Goldsworth, at your service."

"C.C. Tinsley, at yours," he started. "But I suppose you knew that already."

"Yes," Goldsworth said again, a grin sneaking into his voice.

"So," Tinsley prompted after a long awkward silence. "Did your chauffeur lead me here for us to sit in the car or did you want to tell me something? 'Cause I've got work to do."

"No you don't," Goldsworth denounced, the smirk dropping from his voice. "We sent a man to your office while you were searching in vain at the library. You don't have any other cases at the moment, and you don't have any information on us. So, detective, you are lying when you say you have other work, and I do not like being lied to."

Tinsley sat speechless, trying and failing to keep his jaw from dropping. Who did this man think he was? When he had finally thought of something to say, he was interrupted by Goldsworth tapping on the glass of the car window. As way of answering, the chauffeur slid into the driver's seat and pulled the car out of the alley, all the time Goldsworth's face was obscured.

"Where are we going?" Tinsley asked, feeling a bit like a lost child.

"Mr. Beardsley," Goldsworth paused to gesture to the chauffeur, "is going to take you back to the hovel you call an office, and then, unlike you, I will be attending to my very real work that needs to be done. Covering up a murder like the Black Dahlia is extremely difficult you see."

Tinsley was yet again speechless. Goldsworth had just admitted to covering up a major murder case and he was just checking his cufflinks like this was an everyday occurance.

"You're not serious, are you?" Tinsley demanded, clenching his jaw. "If you are, then there is no way you'd let me walk around with that information in my head."

"I'm being entirely serious, detective," Goldsworth confirmed, the smirk creeping back into his voice. "But if you tell anyone about this, why would there be any reason for anyone to believe you? You're a private eye who smokes too much and drinks so much coffee with whiskey that there should be a cocktail named after you. I mean no offense here - or maybe I do - but you're a nobody, detective. Just a beat-up old tin man who never came back from the war."

Tinsley wished he could choke the life out of the man he shared the car with. He wished that all of what just spilled from Goldsworth's smug mouth was false and was just said to provoke him; but it wasn't, and all he'd be doing would be killing a man in cold blood.

"You know I'm right, my little Tinman," Goldsworth stated, falling silent after. For all his faults, Tinsley knew when to shut his mouth, and now was one of those moments.

As the streets passed and the silent car drew nearer to Tinsley's office, it occurred to him that it was becoming more and more likely that instead of leaving this car alive, he'd be leaving with a bloody bullet hole in his head. Tinsley's palms began to sweat, his eyes frantically searching for signs of a gun on Goldsworth or even Mr. Beardsley. Then again, it might not be either of them to pull the trigger, there may likely be someone waiting for him when they arrived.

A thought struck him like a bolt of lightning. Francesca was still at the office. The poor girl had just been hired as a secretary and was probably going to have to either witness her boss being killed or may even be dead herself if someone had indeed been there.

The car slowed to a stop, heightening Tinsley's panic. Mr. Beardsley stepped out without turning the car off; not a good sign. The evening sun came at an angle through the front window that it illuminated Goldsworth's face for the first time throughout their meeting; another bad sign.

"Well," Tinsley muttered, putting all his courage into staring into Goldsworth's deadened black eyes. "This is where I leave you."

"Yes, it is," Goldsworth replied, bored. "Please make this the last time, I do not wish to see you again."

Tinsley's door was opened at that exact moment, almost as if on cue, and he fought to release the sigh of relief that was so desperately trying to escape. He was a grown man, dammit. He had fought the Krauts in Italy and France but couldn't handle a little car ride? What was he becoming?

He had his hand on the doorknob ready to unlock it, when he heard Goldsworth's voice one last time from the car behind him. "If we catch you snooping in our business again Tinman, I might just have to kill you."

Tinsley didn't answer, but instead slid his key into the lock and hoped the car drove away. Panic had crept back into his chest as he flashed back to the war, remembering what it looked like to see a man get shot in the head. Not a pretty sight to say the least, and he had no desire for that to be his fate.

"Welcome back, sir," Francesca greeted when Tinsley entered the room. "Did you find anything?"

"No, just another dead end," he lied, walking past her to his desk to pour himself a cup of coffee and whiskey. He wasn't going to let this go, he couldn't. He had just gotten an unprompted confession and a death threat. However frightening it may be, he would have to run the risk of investigating further.

The days bled into weeks as Tinsley came across more

and more dead ends. There had been no word from Ricardo or anyone who was on the Goldsworth payroll.

Until this morning.

The lights were on at the office when Tinsley arrived, meaning that Francesca was on time for once. The hairs on his neck and arms stood straight. The day Fran was on time was the day the earth changed its rotation. Something was off.

"Fran?" he called when he unlocked the door. "Are you here?"

Drawing the sidearm he bought after the run in with the Goldsworths, he crept around the corner and was met with a sight that no man need ever see.

Francesca was laid out on her desk in two parts, her lifeless eyes clouded with blood. A file was set neatly on her chest displaying the autopsy report of the Black Dahlia. It didn't take a detective to figure out that Francesca's wounds would be eerily identical. Above the body however, was the clearest message of all.

Written on the wall in what was most likely Francesca's blood were the words: "I warned you, Tinman."

Tinsley's arms lay useless at his sides, his gun slipping from his fingers. There was no possible way that this could get any worse, until the cold metallic feeling of a gun barrel lightly touched the back of his head.

"Ricardo?" Tinsley assumed.

"You guessed right, Tinman," he confirmed. "And what

did I tell you about looking into my family?"

"You told me you might just have to kill me," Tinsley answered, trying to keep his voice level and breathing even.

"Correct again," Goldsworth shouted.

He dragged the gun down to Tinsley's neck and circled around to stand in front of him. Blood was splattered across his face and his eyes seemed to be the same macabre color. The smile that stretched his olive toned face was terrifying.

"I'm feeling quite generous today, so I'm going to allow you to live. On one condition," Goldsworth sneered.

The detective took a moment to think before answering. He was good at what he did, so good that he ended up pissing off a crime family so much that they do this. This fact coupled with live or die decision being presented, there was only one possible thing Goldsworth could be talking about.

"You want me to work for you, don't you?" Tinsley guessed, sweat tickling the back of his neck.

Goldsworth paused to take a satisfied breath, his hand unwavering and let one word slip from his lips: "Yes."

"No," Tinsley blurted before even considering what his other option was.

"You're being coy right?" Goldsworth sighed. "You can't actually wish to die instead of working for one of the most powerful families in the country. Consider your options here Tinman. On the one hand, you get set up with a house in a neighborhood of your choosing, never want for anything and do what you do best, detect things," he stopped for a moment to whack Tinsley on the cheekbone with the barrel of his gun, causing Tinsley to fall to his knees. "On the other hand, I kill you and make it look like you mutilated dear Fran then popped yourself. The whole scene would look an awful lot like a full confession to the murder of the Black Dhalia, making dear Dr. Hodel a free man. Your choice."

Tinsley was silent for a moment, cradling his face as blood seeped out of his wound. He would be set for life. No more needing to worry about rent, or when he would next eat, or waiting on his next case. All he would need to do was join up with an organization with dubious morals who just killed his secretary and only friend. His breathing faltered as he realised what his answer needed to be.

"What would you need me to do for you?" Tinsley questioned, stalling the inevitable.

"Now you're thinking!" Goldsworth burst sending a swift kick into Tinsley's gut, sending the detective fully to the floor. "We would need you to dig up dirt on people when we feel the need to have information. None of them would be nearly as impossible to find as we were. But I must admit, your spunk was admirable and that's why we contacted you."

"Why don't you just kill me then? If my 'spunk' was so noticeable?" Tinsley coughed out, immediately regretting it.

"I like you, Tinman," Goldsworth confessed, crouching down and grabbing a handful of Tinsley's hair resting the barrel of his gun just below his eye. "You entertain me, and you're good at what you do. So good in fact, you piqued our interests so much that I came to find you." Goldsworth lightly slapped

Tinsley's cheek with the gun emphasizing the word 'you'.

This was humiliating, but nothing near the posthumous desecration of his name if he declined this tempting offer. Goldsworth was right again, and Tinsley knew it.

"Alright," he conceded. "I'll do it."

"Good," Goldsworth smiled. "Welcome to the family."

Chat About It

By Katharine Rottach (Finalist)

9,999.

That was the total amount of chatlogs Myrielle held. 9,999 times she had consciously opened her mouth and spoken to another person in the past three years. 9,999 times she had waited patiently for the required ten minutes to pass. And, befitting for her 9,999 chatlogs, she held 9,999 Chatters. Today was finally the day for her to reach the big one-oh.

She wanted her ten-thousandth chatlog to be something...special. Her mother said the ten-thousands blur together after a few decades, but she clearly never discovered the audio recording feature of the Namons. Regardless, Myrielle needed to find someone to chat with. She wanted her .1% purchasing discount—money off of everything she bought—and dammit she was going to get it.

Ignoring the irritating chat invitations on her wrist's Namon the woman continued her brisk walk towards her destination: the local cafe. She was to meet with a close friend in precisely two minutes for her final Chatters chatlog of the day. They would record a verbal conversation, buy coffee, and split separate ways—just before the discount applied and a small part of her life changed.

The door automatically opened once she drew near the entrance. The scent of fresh coffee assaulted her nostrils while she moved out of the way to search for Chloe. Upon seeing her, Myrielle quirked a smile and advanced towards the small table. She tapped Chloe's laptop shell and waited for a response. Without a word, Chloe held out her wrist. Myrielle followed suit and allowed the Namons to scan and recognize each user's Chatters account. They both beeped and the timers started to count. As if on cue, Chloe rose, lightly shut her laptop, and plastered on a smile.

"Hey, Myrielle!" She exclaimed, drawing out her syllables. Without pausing for a verbal greeting back, Chloe started walking towards the short line of patrons waiting to order. "So I heard that you wanted to have a 'special' chat today, huh? Personally, I don't see what's so wrong with our previous chats, but whatever floats your boat I guess. I already typed my order out for coffee, do you want me to type yours too?"

"Yeah, that should be fine. Order me a small iced coffee." Myrielle joined her friend in line. "Oh, and yeah, I do want to record our chat for today. Having ten-kay Chatters is a big deal for this early on, ya know? My older brother pranced around for four years before he even reached five-kay! So, anyway, I was reading online about someone who had a 'special conversation' with their dad when they reached fifty-kay. And I thought, 'What's wrong with having one this early on?' And here I am. In front of—well, uh, actually behind you."

Chloe nodded along at the right points. "That seems fair. So, what exactly counts as a 'special' chat? I assume it's something out of the ordinary and whatnot, something to fit that 'special' label."

Myrielle paused, twisting a curl in thought. "Well," she began. "you know how we always talk about whatever? The article said we should actually, like, develop questions or something. I mean obviously, we're already asking questions, but I mean...'deep questions,' I think the article called them. Eye-dee-kay what they mean by 'deep' though. Maybe bigger questions?"

The woman glanced down at her Namon; 2:57. Just less than ten more minutes until her .1% off discount!

Chloe hummed. "Bigger questions, right. But then what counts as a bigger question? Technically we could say that a long verbal sentence counts as a bigger question as long as a question mark is at the end, but then what does the question talk about?" She blinked in surprise. "Did I—did I just use a question in my own statement to prove my point? Oh, did I do it again? I think I did it again! Oh, that is fun!" She giggled in joy.

Myrielle nodded hesitantly. That...really wasn't funny, she thought.

She was about to open her mouth to reply when they reached the cashier. Silence fell between them. The cashier blinked tiredly and gestured for a phone. Chloe pulled up the ordering app and the employee scanned the barcode. The nearby computer beeped and the worker nodded in thanks. The two of them moved to the side of the counter and waited for the drinks. When the Namons beeped warningly—they hadn't detected words in thirty seconds—Chloe immediately began to ramble.

"So just the other day I was heading into town and I saw the cutest dress in that shop over by that one pizza place near...'Oh-em-gee, that's so cute, I need it.' And I didn't really wanna...but it was just. So. Cute. So I headed into—"

Myrielle, who usually paid attention to Chloe's impromptu bursts of speech, found herself slowly frowning. This didn't seem like the "special" chat she desired. What did shopping have to do with Chatters? Moving from a .09% discount to a .1% discount was sort of a big deal; it was more free money after all! Before she knew it every item she bought would be 1% off of its original price. Oh, to be in the future.

Her saving grace from the blabbering was a buzzing from her friend's Namon. The time it took for the drinks to be picked up was just long enough for Myrielle to open her mouth and ask her question.

"Chloe, no offense to you oh-eff-see, but, uh, what do clothes have to do with my Chatters?"

The opposing woman blinked once. Twice. Then, a lightbulb went off. "Ohhhhh, I forgot you wanted your chatlog recorded! I was just trying to get you your discount, so if anything you should be thanking me. But if you still wanna ask me questions, go ahead."

Myrielle sighed in relief. "Thanks. I was wondering if—"

She cut off upon seeing the glowing numbers on her wrist.

11:09.

10,000.1.

A Hound and His Master

By Everette Brousseau (Finalist and Honorable Mention)

The bloodhound watches from the hearth as his master and his guest converse. His coat is brown, black on his back and round his muzzle. His skin sags in folds, giving his face a droopy, melancholy look, but his doleful eyes peer adoringly at his master.

"Duke's the finest bloodhound in England," he is saying. "He can find a scent in a second, and he'll follow until the animal drops."

At the sound of his name, the hound's ears perk, his tail thumping the ground.

"Perhaps he is no better than my own dogs," the other nobleman replies.

"A challenge then? How about a competition in a fortnight?"

The companions agree upon a time, place, and a list of invites, noblemen with dogs deemed worthy of competing in the hunt, and the conversation turns, murmuring deep into the night until the fire's snapping dies into the sleepy glow of coals.

The air is warm, a few wispy clouds in the sky. The world is sleepy, lazily blinking in the mid-summer sunshine. In contrast with the drowsy summer day, the hounds bound about in excitement, making the horses nicker nervously. Once the men are mounted, and the signal given, the hounds sniff the air. Duke, the first to find a scent, bounds off, leading the pack of baying hounds. They race into the forest, the men on horses behind.

To Duke, the world sharpens as excitement courses though him. Bushes strike his legs, trees blur overhead. He can smell rich soil, decaying leaves, sunlight and wind, and ahead, his prey. He focuses on the smell of the prey and the longing to please his master. He sprints faster, pushing himself a few bounds ahead of the group. His prey is so tantalizingly close. The distance between him and the group lengthens further. And now he can see it: the shape crashing through the underbrush ahead. He runs faster; the pack of hounds is soon many yards behind.

Adrenaline surges through the wild boar. She blunders through bushes and thickets, the cry of the hunting hounds gaining behind her. Spotting a rocky ledge and plunging drop ahead, she stops, desperately turning to face the solitary hound ahead of its group. The whole pack is quickly approaching; the boar knows if she does not escape this hound and keep running, she will be trapped. As she attempts to dart past the hound, it leaps into her path, growling. Frantic, the boar charges the dog, barely hearing the snap of it leg and its yelp. Yet the determined dog dances, limping on three legs, in front of the boar, snapping at her throat. And then the howling pack arrives, forming a semi-circle around the terrified boar, bringing her to bay against the sharp drop.

Led to the prey by the baying of the hounds, the noblemen thunder up on their horses. The sound of a shot pierces through trees, and then the boar lies, motionless in the dirt, as silence descends on the woods. As the men dismount to inspect their kill, Duke sinks to the ground, whimpering. His master approaches, crouching down beside him. Duke's tail miserably thumps the ground.

"It seems that Duke is perhaps not the finest hound there ever was," remarks his master's friend, standing beside Duke.

"He was injured because he was ahead of the pack, and therefore, the finest dog," his master replies.

"Regardless, he'll be useless now."

"He may heal," Duke's master sighs.

The bloodhound spends the following days curled by the hearth. Whenever his master walks by, he thumps his tail, hoping for a pat or a kind word, but he is mostly ignored, and his ears droop in despair, his eyes mournfully following his master's movements. Forlorn, he watches Autumn paint the trees red; he hears the winds moaning, and the birds crying overhead, fleeing from the cold. He smells the frosts approaching, and slowly, he heals. First, he manages to stand, and then limp a few steps. Soon, he is following his master around, eyes begging for attention.

But swiftly it becomes clear that his leg will never heal properly; he'll never again run fast enough for the hunt. His master regards him coldly, and the hound despairs, wishing only to please his master and hunt again.

"Come, Duke."

After so many weeks of being ignored, the bloodhound, hearing those familiar words and seeing his master, gun in hand, step out into the chill, windy day, springs to his paws in joy, bounding outside after the man, forgetting his limp. As his master saddles his horse, the dog limps about in the browning grasses, tail wagging, scenting the chill air. When his master mounts, the hound hobbles towards the meadow where they always start their hunts, gusts of nipping wind flapping his long, floppy ears, whirling the fallen leaves along the ground like ethereal dancers dressed in red, orange, and gold.

The trees, set ablaze by the quick breath of autumn, flame against the clear sky. Duke lifts his nose, scenting the air. He smells the dying grasses and knows a deer has been through recently. He barks, looking back toward his master as he follows into the field. He is ready for the hunt.

When his master dismounts, the hound, confused, trots over, uncertainly licking his master's hand. In a few efficient movements, the man loads his gun, and the hound sits back on its haunches, head cocked to one side, waiting for the signal to start the hunt. The man levels his rifle at the dog. As he stares down the barrel of the gun, the hound's ears droop, and he whines softly; he knows what the gun does.

67

The shot echoes against the tree trunks and resounds against the hard, unforgiving sky. Then, only the wind can be heard, a last lament that twirls its spirited, mourning dancers across the ground and sobs away, as the body of the dog shutters once, and then stills.

Chasing Heaven

By Alicia Morelos (Finalist)

No, I didn't kill her. Murder is a cold-blooded and brutal act. I gave her peace. Her life was a swirling wind of devastation which caused her excruciating pain, but I took her into my arms. I made her feel safe, kissed her, then said goodbye. I am at such a loss without her. She used to be so graceful; The most divine piece of art that ever walked upon this grass. It has been thirty-seven years since my life sentencing and not one day has passed without her crossing my mind. For hours, I would sit up pondering the thought of laying next to her once again as our hands move across the coarse grass and into each other's warmth. My life is a small price to pay to feel that once again. I hope the prison guards don't notice me gone before then. Walking through this forest is so calming; Perhaps it is that sweet earthy aroma. As I continue on this familiar path, the tranquility between these trees begins to fade. Loose branches crackle and the leaves on bushes rustle every so often. Although odd, I pass it off as the wind. I finally reached the hill that we used to come to every Friday night. This is where we had our first date, our first fight, and where we first connected. This is where she took her last breath and where I will take mine. I take in the beautiful scenery. As I am about to reach into my bag for my G19, I am interrupted by a child's voice. "You look like my grandpa." I turned around to discover that the voice belonged to a dark haired little girl with dirt stains all over her face and light pink dress. I take a glance around to see if anyone else is near. "Where are your parents?"

She takes a seat next to me. "I haven't seen them in days... They do that sometimes."

"Do what?"

"Leave." She pauses and takes a brief look at my bag. "Do you have any food?"

I go into my bag and take out a half-eaten chocolate bar to give to her. Her face lit up and quickly took the bar out of my hands. It became apparent to me that her neglectful parents didn't concern themselves with feeding her. I wonder if she knows how unfortunate her living conditions are. Once she is done eating, she begins to look at my face as if she were studying me. "Did you come back from heaven?" she asked.

"I'm sorry?"

"Mommy told me that my grandpa moved to heaven and you look a lot like him."

I glance back at my bag and then turn to look at the little girl.

"I'm actually headed to heaven right now. Maybe, I will see your grandpa there."

"Can I go with you?"

It took me a moment to process her question. I take another look at my bag then stand up with confidence.

"Let's go."

We walk off leaving the bag behind. I have no idea what I am doing or why I am doing it but for the first time, I felt like there was a purpose that I needed to fulfill. I took the little girl with me to Arkansas. Far away from our home state to hide away from our past.

Six months later:

Millie Harriot: The seven-year-old girl who gave my life meaning. She is the reason I wake up every day. Because of her, I discovered a love that I never knew existed. Her birth parents took her for granted. How could they be so cruel and irresponsible? They don't deserve her. I make sure she eats every day. I make sure she is always in clean close. I make sure she is safe. I make sure she knows that I love her. She knows we aren't related, but she thinks of me as her second grandpa. Because of this, she started calling me baba. I know I only met her a couple of months ago, but I can't picture my life without her. It is currently eight in the morning, and I am about to wake Millie up to proceed with our exploration. Ever since we met, we have dedicated a few days out of the week to look for heaven. I always wake up just a few minutes before Millie to scatter clues around every hotel we stay in, to make her believe that we are on an exploration. One day, I will tell her the truth, but right now I just want her to be a kid and enjoy her childhood. I go over to Millie and shake her until she is awake. "Are you ready to go explore?" I asked her. Although tired, she gives out a huge smile and nods. "Okay but after breakfast." We go down for the free breakfast that the hotel has to offer and then go back upstairs for the next clue. It read "Leave the hotel and find the nearest bus station." Millie was the most excited she has ever been since this exhibition commenced. "We're close baba, I can feel it" she exclaimed. We walked for two blocks until we finally saw a bus station across the street. Millie took off from my side. I saw headlights heading in her direction. Time slowed down. My heart pounded violently. I sprint after her. The tires squeal... It's too late. At this moment I felt my heart rip out of my chest and brutally smash onto the harsh pavement. I hold her tightly in my arms and let out a deafening screech.

One month later:

It wasn't long until officials discovered my identity. I was arrested and additionally charged with kidnapping and escape in the first degree, but what does that matter? Nothing. I represent a vessel for nothing. I am nothing. Only one thing is certain; Millie found her heaven.

Grandfather Clock

By Edison Luttrell (Finalist)

You would sit on the floor and listen to Grandpa read stories as the grandfather clock stood overhead, seemingly ticking and tocking with every word and adventure he described. The years would fly by but Grandpa's house would always be your safe haven, listening to his story's about meeting your grandmother, about the trips and wacky adventures and mischief that he would get into in his younger years, all while protected from the outside world with the slow swinging eyes of the old grandfather clock.

Every week after you finish your part-time job, you would go over to your Grandpa's house to check in and make sure that he's eating well and to make sure he's ok, you would laugh together as you would tell him of some mishaps from work and he would tell you some of his, it was quiet and good-hearted, and always in the background, you could hear the ticking of the old grandfather clock.

After your Grandpa would have had to miss your

wedding you would go and pay him a visit, showing him photos of his granddaughter-in-law. He laughs weakly as he would tell you about his own wedding and how he didn't know what to say, how he stuttered during his vows, how he spilled cake all over his suit. You've heard these stories before but you know it makes him happy and so it does the same to you. Your Grandpa's slowed breathing is on beat with the soft alarm of the old grandfather clock.

Even more years later you are sitting by his hospital bed grasping his hand as if it would help keep his life where it is, but he just smiles and puts his other hand up to your face wiping away the tears rolling down your face. He said softly "don't worry, I knew that this would happen eventually, our time together is like those old books I used to read to you as a child, I loved every second of it, but eventually, you had to hit the cover and end the story." He laid back coughing gently. "Remember, a story is more than just words, it's the way to make moments to connect with those you love." He took a deep breath in and exhaled slowly as the beeping on the monitor slowly became steady and unending.

To this very day, you go to the old house and sit underneath the old ticking and tocking of the grandfather clock, but instead of the safety and comfort it once brought, it gave you grief and sadness as you cry, wishing for the ability to turn back the grandfather clock's hands and go to those magical stories you once loved.

And She Smiled

By Emily Seaver (Finalist and Honorable Mention)

She smiled. He smiled back. This was love, wasn't it? She fit perfectly into his arms, her head resting on his shoulder. She'd run her fingers along his jaw, across his neck where the stubble grew just thick enough to prick her. And he couldn't stop smiling when she was around. Yes, this was love. He knew it.

In the beginning, metalworking bonded them. The scorching flames reminded him of the heat in his cheeks when they first met. He'd stuttered out a greeting. She'd smiled her radiant smile and the two were swept up into a love story that bordered on a year now. When they met he'd shown her the knives he created in his backyard forge, and she asked if she could make one. It took him three tries to get an affirmation out coherently. She wasn't bothered by his stutter, but smiled again and agreed upon a time.

When she arrived, the workshop lay clean and tools polished, ready for creating. Hours of sweat and a bucket of laughter produced a perfect knife. He couldn't help but smile at the gleam in her eyes as she held the blade up in the light. She was so proud. And he was proud of her. He loved her.

A few months later he was looking for a ring.

He had mentioned it to her once, but she insisted a ring didn't matter, that they could wed without all the traditional gaudy symbols. He frowned. Of course they would do it the way it had always been done. He loved her and he wanted to provide everything she needed. She'd thrown her arms around him, stroked his cheek, ran her fingers down the side of his neck and followed his collarbone. The light illuminated her eyes emerald green. That was the first night he kissed her.

The second time they kissed followed her presentation of the knife for him to clean. When he first saw the crimson-covered metal, terror seized him. With a blush, she admitted to slaughtering a chicken in an attempt to recreate the French guillotine.

Although unease twisted his stomach, he cleaned the knife, sharpened it, and made her promise never to recreate history again. Then he walked her home. She shouldn't have been out this late. Didn't she know college was close to the slums? Her blush deepened. In the light of a streetlamp, she glowed. Green eyes and black ringlets framed her face in a halo, like she was some dark angel. With a whispered permission she was swept into another fantastic kiss, her hands caressing his Adam's apple and his arms around her waist.

He bought the ring that night. She would love it-- it was traditional in all ways except the ruby, crimson and glowing, where the diamond should have been. It was her favourite colour, exciting, adventurous, daring. He always complimented her whenever she wore her adored blood-red blouse. That night, too, he realized that she never talked about her parents. Was there anyone he should request her hand from? When mentioned, she shrugged it off. Compassion flooded him. That must be why she desired to break traditions. She must have suffered under parents who followed old rules. Maybe he shouldn't have bought the ring. Well, it was too late now and at the worst they could resell it for something she liked.

The day she came running to him across the campus, he realized where he'd propose. She clutched a flier for the state fair in her fist. Her eyes glowed with excitement as she tumbled over her words. She'd been to a fair once as a child but never rode the rides. Could he take her please? He grinned in response. Yes, of course he would take her. They could go together and ride-- what was it? Ah, yes, the Widow's Web. If she wanted it, he'd give her everything and more.

On the agreed day nervousness tickled his thoughts. He pocketed the ring, hopped in the car, and took a deep breath. Perfection was mandatory. He wanted to show her how much he loved her. This was love, and he longed to show it.

When he arrived at her house, she climbed into the car with a smile and blue jean shorts and her favorite red blouse flowing around her torso. The little box in his back pocket dug into his buttox. He wished he'd put it in his front pocket, except she'd see it and she couldn't know what he was up to. If only he owned a handbag like the one she clutched to her chest. It was a deeper red than her shirt, leather, and glinted in the setting July sun. Her lips pulled apart in a slow smile and her fingers twitched. He asked if she was nervous. Yes, she was. Did she know what he had planned?

They got out of the car and paid for their tickets and spent the evening riding every ride until she no longer shrieked in excitement at the thrills of up and down. Then he grabbed her hand and pulled her into an alley. Her eyes glinted. He leaned forward to kneel but she clutched him in a hug, ridiculously strong for her small form. She sunk into him, and him into her. One of her arms slipped from his side and pulled something from her purse. The other hand traced his collarbone. It was time for another kiss, he knew. He leaned towards her but before their lips met something cold followed the warmth where her fingers touched. A boiling liquid poured itself down his throat, choking him.

He collapsed as the liquid filled his lungs. He grabbed at his neck but the liquid spilt over his hands. He looked up at her, at the red on the knife. The knife he had made with her. She wiped it on her blouse. Green eyes glinted as his vision blurred with white. And she smiled.

The Casanova

By Jasmine Redo (Finalist)

The Prologue:

The Casanova.

He was a clever foe, known from far and wide.

He's given rules but never abides1.

He has a distinct walk and talk,

So people tend to gawk.

He can make his personality as sweet as you please2.

And his favorite place to travel was Belize.

He's annoying as a flea,

But for some reason when people see him they light up with glee.

His arms droop low to the floor because when he works out he gets sore.

His smile is nice but he's rotten to the core3.

His face is symmetrical and his features are aligned

And with that people find him certainly divine.

People adore his charm and tend to stick by his arm,

So that alone should spark an alarm.

When he speaks he tends to lie4,

for he is sneaky and you can tell by the spacing between his eyes.

He can manipulate with ease so people never realize that he's a tease.

His looks are so pleasant that people see him and freeze.

The tale:

Sometime ago, there was a man that went by the name of Casanova D.

He was an all American football player that graduated from Florida State University

and married his college sweetheart.

He went on to be a financial advisor with a knack

for investing money. Now, this isn't the average

American Greed story as you will soon see.

Right now it looks like he is as happy as can be.

He started his job by investing other peoples' money.

People thought he was a good guy, but over the years

this all became a lie. He pretended to invest,

but he was only interested in himself.

He lived off of the money he stole1

with a big house and expensive cars. He had a yacht,

so you can see he is living over the top.

But his house of cards began to crumble

when his co-workers decided to mumble.

They were all broke and struggling to pay rent and they started to ask themselves

"How is Casanova D making more money than me?"

The rumors started to spread and then someone called the feds.

As the pressure began to mount he planned to flee the country

with the money in his account. Now, you may be wondering how he can leave,

when he has a baby and wife that have needs. But, his life was at stake and

he realized he made a mistake. So, while everyone was asleep, he packed his bags and did the dash.

It might sound insane but he hopped on a plane,

while it started to pour down rain.

He landed in Belize and found a house in a breeze.

Two years later, he remarried a woman named Sadie,

but that's kind of shady when he knew he had a lady

and a child named Katie back home3. He was quiet for a while,

but that's not his style, so he eventually went back to his old, crooked ways.

He ran for prime minister and I know that's kind of sinister,

but that's just the game he plays. He had a big appeal like a fancy automobile

and this helped him seal the deal for his political race2.

Once he won, he stood stunned as citizens did anything he pleased.

But one day he was feeling kind of nauseous while he was sitting in his office,

because of a drink he just took. He started feeling dizzy

and looking a bit silly and ended up tumbling to the ground.

Later he woke up and almost had a stroke, because sitting in front of him

was his ex wife that seemed pretty provoked. Standing by her side were trained police and enraged victims. His heart began to pound as his reign came tumbling down.

He started to tell lies because he was running out of replies

and a proper excuse to give4. The police arrested him and put him in jail without bail.

Now, he permanently resides in an 8 by 10 foot cell.

The end.

Footnotes Explained:

(1): In the prologue I state "He's given rules but never abides1" and in the story I back this up by talking about how he steals peoples' money and uses it for his own benefit, which is illegal. He also lies to the police, which in some situations can be considered illegal.

(2): In the prologue I state "He can make his personality as sweet as you please2 " and in the story I explain how his appeal helped him win the election.

(3): In the prologue I state "His smile is nice but he's rotten to the core3" and throughout story I talk about how he has done awful things such as, steal money from innocent people and leave his wife and child with nothing.?

(4): In the prologue I state "When he speaks he tends to lie4" and it is apparent that he lies to get out of the tough situation he is in when he gets caught and he has lied to his clients about what he has really been doing.

How I failed Algebra 2

By Lisset (Finalist)

It was a normal day in school, the bell rang and we walked to our 5th period. I walked into my Algebra 2 class. I wasn't excited to be in the class and sit down to listen to the lecture. So as soon as I walked in, I grabbed the sheets of paper that sat on the table next to the door, took my seat and put my head down. I did this every single day of my sophomore year, leading me to retake the class my junior year.

So what led me to be in Algebra 2, yet again? Well, I wouldn't do my homework because I thought it wouldn't impact my grade. I wouldn't try in quizzes because I told myself I could just retake the quiz but never did. I would put my head down because I'd see my friends do it too. By the end of the year, I was told I required an 88 to pass the class. My teacher gave me a packet of homework I could do to boost my grade; I decided not to do it. Later on, I was informed I could do online summer school instead of retaking the whole class and I told myself, "Lisset, you're going to do online summer school for sure!" but I didn't. I had the mentality of thinking "Oh, it doesn't matter. They're still going to pass me." In school I had an hour for lunch, I could have taken 30 minutes to sit down and do it, I could've gone to tutoring with my algebra teacher. Instead, I was "busy" strolling and gossiping with my friends, let's not forget amused with watching pranks on youtube.

By the time junior year came, I had a dissimilar mentality. I walked in, not thrilled, but I picked up my worksheet by the door, sat down and did my work. The teacher gave the lecture and then we had independent practice and I made sure to try and finish the whole worksheet. Whenever I didn't understand something, I made sure to raise my hand and ask for help. Since we had a late dismissal time and I had other things to do at home, I made sure that during my free time in school I took some time to do my homework, even if the due date had passed. I still tried to turn it in. And you bet I did my best in unit tests and quizzes.

What I learned from this experience is to try my hardest and not be irresponsible because if I want to get somewhere big in life I have to focus on myself and not what others do because, at the end of the day, it's going to be my choices, my grade, and my life. I also acknowledged the value of education, and I'm grateful to have access to it because so many people who wish to have it, don't have this chance.

False Reality

By Reagan Phelps (Finalist)

The night was cold, but my soul is what was frigid. It felt like eons, the time that I'd spent on this road, my eyes locked on the license-plate of the black Chevrolet Bel-Air that I chased. Never getting any closer, time stretching forever. The straight black road I drove was slick with water, yet it hadn't rained; the engine of the car I chased roared, yet the silence in my own mind was all the more deafening; I'd been driving for what felt like eternity, yet I hadn't moved. These thoughts, these stifling contradictions, they ravaged my mind indefatigably until I was forced to ponder the point of existence, the point of what I was doing and the car I was driving.

It was this search for a purpose that led me to realize what I'd feared for quite some time- that I didn't know who was in the black Bel-Air ahead of me, barely visible through a window of fog, or why I was compelled to chase them.

My mind, it was broken, shattered like a glass, as I'd

forgotten my very purpose- though I'm not sure I ever knew that in the first place. What I did know is that I could never stop driving on the empty, dark road of time. Not until the car ahead of me was caught.

I also knew that this wasn't some newfound epiphany, but rather something that has always been in the back of my mind, unwilling to make itself apparent; In my empty mind, I likened it to memorizing a song, but only humming the melody, ignoring the words that should pursue. I went over this bittersweet idea in my head repetitively, taking hours of my never-ending time to consider it. Perhaps this is because I knew the minute I let go of it, my thoughts would be empty again and it would be forgotten, lost in the emptiness of what is left behind, the remnants to a sparked fire. Nonetheless, the ashes of this idea were soon swept away anyways, as my mind became occupied with something else. Something that I again was fairly aware of, but only chose to bring to my own attention now. I gripped the steering wheel tighter as my mind was submerged with speculation.

My soul, as I mused, was frozen and had been for quite some time; and yet the chill that swept from my brain to the foot that pushed against the pedal at the floorboards was something I couldn't describe or recognize- for it only came upon the moment my blood-shot eyes moved from the license-plate of the shiny black car and shifted, an action I had no recollection of doing ever before. The entire extent of this journey on the road, I'd stared. Stared, at the car with an unknown driver; the car who I felt was my only purpose to chase, but who I'd never reach; the car who was the only thing my mind knew; the Bel-Air ahead of me who was the only other moving thing in this empty place. Or so I thought.

As I had previously mentioned, the time I'd been in this car I drove was undefinable, and I didn't know how long it'd been. What I did know is that in the time it had been, never had I taken my eyes off of the license-plate of the car- I wasn't even aware I had the ability to. Perhaps I never had this ability until that very moment, or perhaps I'd always possessed it, simply unwilling to do so in fear of seeing something I didn't want to. This consideration made me uncomfortable, and I allowed it to be swept away.

But oh, how I laugh at the irony in this. For what I saw upon moving my eyes was all the more unsettling. They fixated on the closest thing they could settle on- the rear-view mirror.

But they were met with blinding light.

This nauseating light belonged to another car whose headlights shone through the rear-window of my car and into my eyes. My thoughts were confused, and further my glass mind broke.

There was another car.

Another black Chevy Bel-Air, another lost soul (chasing) on this endless road, behind me the same distance that I was behind the car ahead of me who'd consumed my existence for so long, but now seemed significantly less important. I returned my gaze to this car in hopes of finding comfort in it's familiarity.

But it was gone.

Now there was only the slick black road that stretched on forever. The road I knew so well, an old friend that changed only in that it now lacked the car I'd been chasing for an eternity. A tear fell down my face.

It fell with the realization that I'd been avoiding for so long, the final thought that confirmed my fears. It fell, as I accepted the knowledge that I've held this span of eons but had pushed away in desperation- it fell, as I accepted that the car I was driving was also a black Bel-Air, and that I'd be condemned to drive it, be "chased" by the driver behind me as I'd chased my precursor.

Perhaps this was Hell- Purgatory, maybe, though I'm not sure I believe that. I killed this thought immediately as I recognized that my days of pondering were over. My freedom was taken, and this road was a prison I would never know why I was in or how to escape from as this was the punishment for whatever actions placed me here. I would drive and be chased, as would the unlucky soul in the car behind me and whoever had once been in the one ahead. My final realization was over, and even thinking was pointless.

Instead, I continued to drive in the shiny black Chevy Bel-Air in the prison of time, feeling nothing besides the frigidity of the night.

And yet, my soul was colder.

SECTION 3 – CHANGE

Copper Penny

By Dakota Kirk (Finalist and Honorable Mention)

They would have dismissed him immediately had they known, but the discovery was not made until years later, and by then, John Miller had retired from the U.S. Treasury Department in Denver, Colorado. It was early in the year 1943 when he received the memorandum from the government, sitting atop a heavy box. He was running late and on his way out the door to go home, preoccupied with the idea of another confrontation with the wife about being late - yet another ridiculous battle they continually had about stiff, cold mashed potatoes; about wilted salads and watered-down lemonades. He pictured her cold stare, her lips pressed together until there was just a thin line upon her sagging face. Sometimes he hated her. He glanced once more at the memo, thought of the wife, and hurriedly locked the door on his way out.

John arrived early the next morning. Perhaps it was his distraction with weekend plans and the dread of spending two days with the wife that had him jumping into his routine, no thought directed at the memo he received the day before. He was preparing the machine for the minting of coins, pennies today. The copper plates gleamed, and he continued to ponder the weekend plans and what hell awaited him as the machine began to warm up and prepare to stamp out the shiny copper pennies. His gaze fell on the paper he had quickly tossed aside the day before, arm shifting to bring the document into his line of sight. As he took in the letters on the page, his finger flew to the stop button of the machine. His eyes darted right to left, taking in the entirety of the document, the paragraphs outlining how the war efforts were priority, that bullets and tanks trumped coins. A new formula had been created and the plates found in the box accompanying the memo were to be inserted into the machines immediately, resulting in the reduction of copper to roughly 2% of the coins' makeup, zinc now making up the majority ingredient. With a worried glance at the machine, Miller realized that his distraction had resulted in the minting of one shiny copper 1943 penny, an error he knew could leave him in the unemployment line. With retirement up around the bend, it was a mistake he couldn't let be discovered. He hurriedly removed the penny, dropping it into his pocket and immediately went to work installing the new plates. On the way home, he stopped in at the local Woolworths, buying a pack of Wrigley gum, three sticks for twelve cents, the dreaded penny in his hand along with other coins making up the difference, ridding himself of the mistake once and for all.

Standing in line behind Mr. Miller was Peggy Sue Flaherty, wishing the cashier would move along – she had to get some rest before her flight to Washington DC in the morning. Peggy was born and raised in DC and was excited for the Spring Break from her studies at Colorado Women's College. Her flight would get in late on Saturday night, then she'd have some down-time before Tuesday, April 13th when she and her family planned to attend the Jefferson Memorial dedication ceremony. With all the unrest in the world related to the war and the distance between herself and her parents, Peggy Sue was more than a little homesick. The man ahead finished his gum purchase. Peggy Sue placed her toiletry items on the cashier stand, made her purchases, and left the store with a shiny copper 1943 penny in her coin purse.

It couldn't have been a more perfect day. On the shore of the Potomac River sat the majestic structure, the dome-shaped roof gleaming in the brightness of the overcast afternoon skies. President Franklin D. Roosevelt stood at the lectern to dedicate this American treasure, the statue of Thomas Jefferson inside a mere plaster cast of what was supposed to be a towering 19-foot statue made of bronze – another victim of the war efforts and its limited supply of precious metal. Peggy Sue stood amongst the nearly 5000 onlookers in the plaza at the base of the white marble steps, her hand shielding her eyes from glaring caused by the afternoon light hitting the white marble all around them. Roosevelt spoke about Jefferson, "He lived in a world in which freedom of conscience and freedom of mind were battles still to be fought through – not principles already accepted by all men. We, too, have lived in such a world." The penny sat neatly in Peggy Sue's coin purse. After the ceremony, she and her parents strolled along the Potomac, Peggy stopping at an ice cream vendor to buy a refreshing single-dip cone for 5c. She transferred the five pennies into the hand of one Huan Hui, a Chinese man who was working overtime as an ice cream vendor, saving every penny he could to treat his family to a Coney Island Vacation. He slipped the pennies into his cash box.

Huan Hui was a man of integrity and honor. He would have been horrified to find out he was the recipient of the forbidden penny. Huan was a prideful man, always aware of the struggle his family had endured so that he could live in the United States. His great-grandfather, Guozhi Hui had made passage to the US in 1848 in search of gold – the California Gold Rush. He quickly learned that not all that glitters is gold and ended up hammering railroad ties into the hard earth under the burning sun to make ends meet and save money to bring his family to the US. The railroad work was intense, and the toll it took on his body was great. Huan thinks of his great grandfather and remembers his mangled fingers from photographs, feeling shame when he recalls how he would recoil from seeing them. Finally, after almost 10-years, Guozhi paid the voyage on a cargo ship for his wife, son, and daughter to join him. It was a brutal trip, one the daughter would not survive and one that Ah Kum, Guozhi's wife, would never heal from. She fell into a pool of depression so deep that she couldn't seem to find a way to paddle to the edge. Guozhi was only grateful they had lost the daughter and not the boy named Fuhua. The boy found himself growing up in a joyless home, so when he was able to find employment and a wife of his own, he couldn't get out fast enough. He quickly had his son, Li Hui, a pleasant enough boy who became the apple of his eye. Huan closes and locks his cashbox, finished for the night. Thousands of miles across the ocean, the United States Air Force rained pamphlets down from the sky to the Japanese below, demanding their surrender or assuring their demise. The US would drop an atomic bomb on Hiroshima the next day.

July of 1944 and the Hui Family Vacation was finally happening, an event they had sacrificed for – saving pennies away over the years. Ju Hui, held tightly to the coin purse that her father had filled with loose change, letting her know that this is what she could use in the arcade of Luna Park and to buy herself sweets from the candy shop. The family would spend the next two days attempting to have fun at the amusement park and the beach while trying to deny the hostile gazes of the white park-goers. Ju wanted to scream from the top of her lungs that she was Chinese, not Japanese. White people didn't care. She cast her gaze to the sand, continued working on the sandcastle she was building. Ju heard a voice shouting, "Lemonade, lemonade!" after a questioning glance to her father and the nod of confirmation, she ran to her change pouch that lay tucked safely beneath her beach towel, cupped it in her left hand and used her right hand to ease the drawstring loose that cinched the sack. She hurriedly tumbled some coins into her sandy palm and then tossed the pouch quickly back under the towel as she raced across the sand to the vendor. At the end of the summer day, Ju gathered up her towel and coin purse, unaware that a single copper penny had fallen and worked itself into the sand below.

Samuel Jenkins considered himself a decent treasure hunter. His wife would say he liked to waste time because his trinkets hadn't amounted to much, after all. Sam couldn't wait to get out on the sand today and try out his new Oremaster Super Geiger Counter, the latest and greatest tube-based metal detector. It had cost him a pretty penny, but surely it would pay for itself in no time. Sam strapped on the gear, seven pounds worth, and proceeded to stroll up and down the shoreline, sweat beading on his forehead from the effort of it all, his skin turning pink under the relentless summer sun. The 4.5" meter was easy to read, the needle moving forward and backward in slight motions, hypnotically rhythmic. Suddenly, a jolt forward: a clear indication that metal was to be found below. Sam eased the strap off his shoulder and lowered the apparatus gently to the sand, loosening the strainer basket and trowel that were clipped to his tool belt. He took scoops of sand and sifted them through, not seeing at first what set off the detector. About a foot down, he saw an unimpressive, dark greenish-grey colored coin which he deposited into the pouch he carried for his finds, then he moved on further down the beach. After getting home and reviewing his loot, Sam wiped off the crusted and eroded sand, saw the coin, and tossed the 1943 penny into a jar with the other non-valuable change he'd found over the years.

Sam died in 1997, his wife Sheila the year after. This created quite a burden for their only son, Samuel Jr. He had to tie up his folk's loose ends and he had no time for it, so he called in an estate sale business to take the load off his plate. Sam came to the property a day before the sale to collect the personal items, photographs and such. He found his father's change jar that held various coins, his jewelry box that held tarnished cuff links. Nothing was of value and he shook his fist in the air thinking about his father, a man who had always kept them in poverty on his search for a big treasure – one that never came. Jr. had escaped that house to head to college and he had never looked back. His poor mother, always scraping to make ends meet, never confiding in Sam Sr. that Jr. would send her money every month just so they could eat and afford the basic necessities. Jr. takes a red-eye flight back home, placing photo albums he took from his parents' home into a drawer, placing the change jar on a bookshelf where it remains for 23 years.

Samuel Jr is watching a TV show on treasures and he swallows his bitterness; this is something his dad would have made him watch and considered it a father/son bonding experience. It's a bit harder to do things now. Sam had to quit working almost 7 years ago and is living on social security income. He tried to plan better – especially after the poverty he faced as a kid. Cancer is a respecter of no one. He had to dip into that change jar yesterday, just to make it through until his check on the 9th. He thinks of life and how unfair it is, how much of a struggle it is, and he wonders if he even wants to continue. Sure – he beat cancer, but the toll it has taken on him is a great one, and his physical disabilities continue to debilitate him. He watches the coins on TV and thinks to himself, "Wouldn't that be the answer to it all? A treasure!" The penny lies in its glass vessel, a beautiful 1943 Indian Head copper penny: worth $150,000. Sam takes a nap.

Leaving My Birthplace

By Habiba Khatun (Finalist)

"Life is short, and we need to make our decisions faster without wasting our time. For this we need support and help which we get from our family and friends all our lives, so we never want them apart." I always want them in every moment of my life weather at my dejection or exhilaration, but it is different from what I desire. Life is a journey and we never know what happens next so we could end up anywhere at any time. Born in a merciful blessed family as a first child with love parents calls me Habiba and I like to introduce myself through my father's name because he always supports me on everything and there is a saying in Bangladesh that "Mayara Babar Kolijar Tukra" (Daughters are the important part of the father's heart). There are events in life, which change us or our way of thinking. As for me, the major changes began through the news to attend the interview in Dhaka.

I remember the day, it was December 17, 2016. As a

regular day, I was getting ready to go to school. The school was half-mile away from my house, so I had to prepare myself early every day because my dad, uses to drop me off, after I am inside the school he could go to his work. In early morning the sound of the bird's songs feels like relaxing deed sleep music. He was known as a member of the union. Therefore, he had plenty of responsibilities, to my dad that job was never challengeable, multiple times I heard him praying to Allah that as he is serving the community, in the same way he could benefit them his rest of the life. From his work, many people outside the group were not happy serval times others told me and to my father to be careful because you never know who has what in their mind. "Habiba don't interrupt your father while he is working, let him keep doing his good work Allah will help us instead" says my mom.

On the morning of shine bright day, slightly a news made my soul like a bright light other side it stretches the mind with the feeling of leaving the I was born. The main time the mail delivery boy came and gave us the mail. On top of the mail, it said an important document inside, my father ripped the edge carefully and noticed that it is from the capital city of Dhaka. Abu (Father) what is it about, why are you seem so pleased, I asked. He replied our dream about to come true, the USA embassy is asking us for an interview. Instead of going to school we went back home and told my mom and little brother Habib about it, by looking at us he became over-excited, but I am sure he had no idea what we were talking about.

My parents had talked about coming here for a very long time, even before I was born. After this news, they started preparing for the interview and started organizing the important documents. This news sounds attractive to me because I am going to see a new city another side sadness about leaving the country. The next day my father call the office for an interview date, they started memorizing names, addresses, also the phone numbers too. My parents knew the officer not going to ask anything to little kids, so I and my brother were tension-free relaxing. One day before the interview date we arrived, and a hotel room was reserved for us, our room was on eight floors, the view of the outside was heavenly gorgeous like a bright star on the clear sky. Next morning, we woke up early than a regular day while they were asking questions, I was paying attention to the pledge which was hanging on the wall then they said our interview was successful and one word he said in Bangla was "Dunnobad" (thanks). The day was one of the happiest days of our lives.

It was a beautiful sunny day, my father announced that we are going to the USA in a month. This sounds outstanding to us and we had a small party for it that night. However, I was excited and impatient to experience a new lifestyle. I realized that I could start a whole new life to make new friends and learn a new language. Additionally, I started feeling nervous because leaving home for opportunities some kind as education, career or even freedom of speech and by thinking of all the great things I have achieved since I was born here. I was thinking to leave the country I reside in to in another nation is going to be a big move, I had a feeling of fear because we are so used to our own culture it might cause a hard time to adopt the new way of living life, all together I was sad for all things that I am no longer going to be able to experience in my day-to-day life, like those people working in the field, the traffic police officers standing by the bus stops, mostly the hug of a family member and other way I was thinking my friends who are such talented and all the people are not able to go and stayed in this less-resourceful state while I am leaving.

The next day I went to school and I was not paying attention to the teacher lectures and my friend Tane asked me 'is everything ok? Did anyone say anything which includes boys?' In Bangladesh schools' boys are more likely to disturb girls' other words it is called eve-teasing; it is like calling their name, troughing love letters on them, touching without permission and public sexual harassment of women by men. I was not answering her and started crying by looking at her concerns for me, because she does not know the reason for me being absent for the last two days. One thing she knew is how to stop my crying, that moment she hugs me tight and asked me slowly:

Tane: What is it that you are hiding from me?

Me: I am leaving you all, I'm going to America. I said

Tane: Good she said with tears in her eyes. When are you going? Are you going to forget me?

Me: End of this month, side by side or miles apart best friends will always be connected by heart I replied.

That day I saw my best friend for last time and till now no see. That moment of salience I could feel future getting shorter and my health declining. Now I don't see them, but I still feel them. The next day I leave for USA, from there a new journey of my life began.

A Good Day

By Sowmya Bulusu (Finalist and Honorable Mention)

'Hi sweetie, how was your day?' Isabella quickly looked for and heard her mom's greeting as her eyes catch her mom while stepping out of the school bus. It was a bit of a crowded bus stop with moms waiting for their children to arrive home from school. It was a long and miserable day for Isabella. Ever since she changed schools after her dad and mom decided to move to a different town, life had changed. School was much simpler last year in sixth grade. The teachers hardly came or gave students any work. And then one fine day during summer, she was told that they were changing homes and moving to a different town because it was better. "Better? No way!" thought Isabella. School was boring last year but boring was better than being miserable!

"You didn't answer my question, sweetie! Is everything okay?" asks mom again. "Okay, I guess!" Isabella murmured. "My teachers are very mean; they give me loads of homework every day. John and Ana have been very unkind to me like they

103

do always. Sue even pushed me harder during our gym class. I have no time to play and I don't have any friends to play with!" Isabella wanted to say the truth but kept it to herself. She noticed her mom looked tired yet held Isabella's hand dearly as they strolled towards their apartment.

As soon as they stepped in, mom helped her wash up and gave her a big hug saying she was very proud of her for going to school, learning and wanting to become a doctor in future. A few tears rolled in her eyes as Isabella couldn't hold her misery anymore. Dad always told her to be brave and that means no tears. Isabella wiped her tears quickly and gave an account of her misery at school to her mom. Mom smiled and told her imagination begins with you, and how tomorrow then becomes better than today and the day before. "Do moms always say this?" wondered Isabella. Mom gets up very early and goes to work and dad gets Isabella ready and drops her at the school bus stop on his way to work only to return very late in the night; sometimes long after Isabella could no longer wait in bed to receive a bear hug and noisy kisses on her forehead. Isabella never understood how tomorrow could be better than today if tomorrow is the same as every other day?

"Imagine just for one day, every experience is wonderful, every person you meet is kind, and see if that makes your tomorrow better", mom suggested as Isabella was falling asleep in her bed.

Isabella got up next morning without her usual complaints and got ready quickly, surprising her dad. The words of her mom still fresh in her head from last night, "Imagine everything is great!" She put on her dress without being grumpy about it looking worn out and dull, and tied her boot laces carefully, even as they looked like they were about to give out at any time. Isabella thought, "Today, I am going to look forward to everything, even if it means I get shoved to the back side of the bus". She smilingly accepted a seat offered by burly Alexi in the rear.

"Your handwriting can be better, and you need to pay more attention to your sentence constructs. Otherwise, you will not improve," remarked the English teacher. Isabella took her comments with a smile and responded earnestly, "Thank you, Mrs. Curtis."

"Isabella go away, your clothes are dirty!" Ana's whisper didn't bother Isabella anymore. She looked at Ana and surprised her with a compliment saying "You look nice in your dress!" and turned away to talk to Miguel. Gym wasn't much distress either as Isabella watched and followed her teacher's instructions to run up and down. She tried as hard as she could to remain enthusiastic throughout the day. Lunch was alright sitting with Jamie, Lee and the frail Chinese twins, Karen and Kathy. The hardest class after lunch was math. Fractions and solving equations seemed tough to handle even on an "Imagine a delightful day" day. But Isabella survived by imagining numbers as nothing but figures that cannot scare her any more, even if they were accompanied with all kinds of symbols wrapped around them. Next was science, taught by Mrs. Bellwether, who resembled a great-grandmother, in thoughts and action. Ciara, her best friend in science, leaned over to inform her a fact that Mrs. Bellwether never married because she hated men. Isabella decided to not pay much attention to the number of times Mrs. Bellwether yawned during class. Instead she started to concentrate on what was being taught - why climate change is directly linked to the meat people eat. Isabella wondered if cows and other animals were left alive, wouldn't they exceed the population of humans in the world? It was social studies next, and despite Mr. McDermott's shouting in class, Isabella appreciated all he was trying to do to get the back benchers his attention.

The closing bell rang and it was time to pack up and go home. Suddenly Isabella felt a connection to the events at school. Boarding the bus, she noticed Ana throw a soft smile at her...or was she just conjuring that up? Isabella walked past the front and middle seats to take a seat next to her bus buddy Alexi, eager to converse about cow population in the world.

"Rosa Park stop!" announced the bus driver, and Isabella hurriedly got up and ran towards the bus door to exit. She quickly looked back to notice the students who were still waiting to be dropped off and felt happy she was getting home sooner. She then walked out to meet her mom. Before her mom could say anything, Isabella whispered into her mom's ears, "I had a good day mom!"

She is a Writer

By Mary Ann M. Panganiban (Finalist and Honorable Mention)

There was once a girl who loved literature. Book, poetry, writing; you name it. She loved it even though she lived in a world where no teenager found it "cool" to even pick up a book. In a world where many deemed it "old-fashioned" because everything was so "modern". But she remained steadfast. If anyone asked about her hobbies, she would always talk about writing with stars in her eyes and a smile on her face. It was a part of her. Balancing life as a writer and a student was something she thought she could handle. 'How hard could it be?' she told herself. She could never imagine a week passing without her jotting down a quick story idea or a short poem throughout her day. The girl never thought she would ever quit writing.

As the new school year started, her schoolwork slowly took up more and more of her time. Studying for A.P. classes, studying for tests, doing homework, managing and leading clubs . . . it took up so many hours that she just set her writing aside, telling herself, I'll do it later. At first, she barely noticed the change in her life, but things pile up as they do. When the amount of work she had to do subsided, she finally decided to sit at her desk with her laptop open. She stared at the blank page in front of her, waiting to be filled with words. 'Seriously?' She thought to herself. 'Why can't I think of anything? Come on, think. You had so many story ideas.' Placing her hands on the keyboard, she tried to type something, but that something never came. With a frustrated sigh, the girl closed her laptop. The document was never opened again.

When anyone asked her about her latest story or poem, she had no response. She had nothing to say when her other friends talked about how much writing they had been up to. The girl felt like her life was empty without writing at first. It was like she was missing something, but she gradually stopped noticing. She found herself having more free time than usual, but she found it hard to try to work on a story or poem. It was as if the writing part of her had disappeared. Hours became days, days became weeks, weeks became months until the months became a year.

When summer finally rolled around, the girl opened her laptop and remembered an old story idea. She started typing until words became sentences, sentences became paragraphs until she had the beginning of a new story in front of her. 'Well,' she thought with a small smile, 'I guess I'm still a writer after all.' A few months passed and the girl found her way to balance all the work she had to do and writing. She finally understood that sometimes writer's block isn't always for a short period of time, but it's something that doesn't last forever. And if anyone asks, she's still a writer.

Good as New

By Jenna McFadden (Finalist and Honorable Mention)

In fourth grade, I had a favorite pair of jeans. My other pairs wouldn't let me climb on the play-structure, or run fast enough to avoid being 'it.' In these, though, I could do cartwheels, jump rope, even touch my toes. I wore them as much as I could and was always disappointed if my mom couldn't get them washed and dried in time for the next day. As the months went on, the fabric around the knees wore thinner with every tumble, and the pockets more threadbare with every acorn. Soon I became over-cautious, scared to fall one more time and ruin my jeans forever. I knew once they were torn, there was no going back.

I still remember the fateful day when my skin first broke through the blue fabric. I was walking the edge of the playground, balancing on the thin border that held in all the bark chips. We'd gotten all the way to the far swings before my left foot found a stray nail sticking out of the wood. I broke my fall with my hands the best I could, but when I looked down— apparently I'd used my knee too. I didn't care that my hands were torn up or that my knee was starting to bleed. I cared that there was a tear through the middle of my favorite pair of jeans.

As soon as I saw my mom's gold minivan pull into the pickup lane after school I ran up to her and jumped in the back seat. "Mom, I need you to fix my jeans."

Once we got home I gave them to her in hopes they'd be returned good-as-new. After examining them for a while, she told me she couldn't resew them. My face fell.

"But," she continued. Maybe there was hope. "We could put a patch over it."

A patch? A patch wasn't what I wanted. I wanted them good as new. I wanted them how they used to be.

The next day I went to school in a different pair of jeans. If I couldn't have my favorite pair, I would just have to make these work. But throughout the day I was constantly reminded of how these were inferior. I sat down at my desk and they rode up to show my ankles. At reading time I couldn't sit criss-cross-applesauce. At recess I couldn't even climb the rock wall.

After school I headed home defeated. Even pedaling my bike the mile home was hard. I parked it in the backyard and started inside. To my surprise, I walked into the dining room and found the dinner table covered in patches. There were birds and dogs and flowers and bees and hearts and everything else you could imagine. I looked up and saw my mom smiling down at me.

"You can pick your favorite patch, then we'll return the rest," she told me.

Originally, this wasn't what I wanted, but the abundance of shapes and colors slowly began to change my mind. Rejuvenated by the hope of wearing my jeans again, I spent the next half hour picking a patch. Eventually, I chose a deep orange monarch butterfly. I helped my mom choose a thread color and position the patch over the wide tear, then watched eagerly as she sewed it on. Was it exactly what I wanted? No, but it meant I could wear my jeans again! And now, they were even cooler than before.

I woke up early the next morning out of excitement. I got to school and showed off my butterfly patch to my friends— who I remember being pretty jealous. That day when I fell doing double-dutch, the patch was tough enough to protect the jeans and my knee. I became brave and fun-loving once more, knowing I had a solution for any tumbles I took. Soon my favorite pair of jeans became the most colorful pair of pants you ever saw, with paw-prints, birds, dogs, you name it. They stood out, which only made me love them more.

The Conversation That Changed Everything

By Brooke Fertig (Finalist)

"Okay Mia, this time we switch, and you play the evil witch," giggled a bright-eyed, young girl. Hands rising as if casting a spell, she flashed a scary, yet goofy look at her companion. "My evilness has its limits," she retorted.

"Oh... um, okay," the other replied with a shy smile, eyes skirting from her companion to the ground. They were seated at the corner of the playground, thoroughly separated from the rest of the children, who were sprinting through the school grounds in massive groups.

A short distance away, a few children stopped in their game to stare. "Why does Mia not make real friends?" a sandy-haired boy questioned.

"Maybe the doctor I overheard the teacher talking about, the one that only talks to her," chimed in a girl whose voice brimmed with curiosity, "will keep making her better, and she will want to play with us one day."

The third child, a red-headed, fair skinned girl, briefly locked eyes with Mia across the playground. "She has gotten better," she added, both she and Mia lightly smiling, "and she will at least look at or talk to us now instead of just playing by herself."

"Hey," Mia's companion, Olivia, carefully ventured, "you alright?"

Seeming to snap out of a trance, Mia looked at Olivia before softly smiling at the ground. "Do you think maybe we should try and play with the other kids today?" she questioned.

"Maybe," Olivia sadly remarked, "but they never talk to me, ignoring me like I am not there."

Mia perked up slightly, stating, "I will bet it is because I have not seen you as much these last few months."

Grinning, she continued, "if you stay around school more, the other kids will come around."

"What do you mean?" Olivia asked, looking genuinely confused. "I've been at school with you every day," she continued. "We just don't always play together at recess every day, or talk during craft time."

"But....." Mia trailed off. "You started coming to school less a few months ago," she ventured, "and now I only see you two or three times a week."

"No, I am always here!" Olivia protested. A tense silence passed for a few seconds before Olivia quietly and asked, "Mia, on those days where you do not talk to me, is it because you cannot see me?"

"I do not see why," Mia cautiously stated, "because I see you clearly now."

"Let me ask, on Monday when you went picking flowers during recess," Olivia began firmly, "was I there with you?"

"No, of course not. It would have been so much more fun with you there though," the girl wistfully said.

Olivia grabbed Mia's shoulders, locking eyes with her. "When you started seeing me less, a few months ago, as you said," Olivia remarked seriously, "that was when you started going to what your parents called 'therapy'."

Olivia could see the gears turning in Mia's head. "So, you might not be real?" Mia asked, tears brimming in her eyes. "But you are my best friend."

"I may be your best friend," Oliva trailed off sadly, "but I think I am your imaginary friend, too."

A silent understanding passed between them as the two began to sniffle. Mia tried to draw Olivia into a hug, but found she could not feel her comforting embraces like she used to be able to.

"It is time for you to start making real friends," Olivia advised, "so that by the time I am really gone, you will have other friendships as good as ours."

"I am not sure I want other friends," pleaded Mia. "Why can I not just make you stay?"

"Everyone has to move on at some point and find where they truly fit in," Olivia asserted, showing wisdom far beyond someone her age. She rose, and Mia shakily joined her. "Now go, live your life," she said. "Always remember our friendship, but don't look back as you dive into change."

Not knowing how to respond, Mia just hesitantly nodded, turning towards a group playing tag a small distance away. She cast one last look at her best friend, a bittersweet smile filled with gratitude and uncertainty, and began to walk towards the group, waving as the kids saw her. Olivia watched proudly and felt herself fade a little.

How shopping malls came to be

By Kate Sunshine (Finalist)

All the Olympians were invited to a party and Aphrodite. the most beautiful, heard through some gossip that Hestia was not going. She was appalled that Hestia was not going to show off her Olympian status to all the poor mortals.

When Hestia was confronted by Aphrodite, she promised to go for a little bit but Aphrodite said,

"I won't have it."

"Have what?" Hesstia said confused.

"Have an Olympian sister going out to a party like this, " she said pointing at Hesstia's soot stained simple dress.

"What is wrong with my dress ? "

"Nothing dear .....except that you are always covered in soot "

"Yes.... it's my job to tend to the hearth" Hestia said ,tapping her foot

"Let me help you get ready at least, please" Aphrodite begged gorgeously like everything else she did. Hestia gave in and the two goddess went to Hestia's godly closet. After just one glance, Aphrodite screamed "This will not do !"

"Why not ?" Hesita complained

"Because …. We're going shopping" Aphordite declared.

"No, this is too much. I will just go like this," Hestia said pointing to her dress

"NO W---WAY," Aphrodite stammered "to the chariot" One moment later , "Where to my ladies?" asked the chariot chauffeur.

"Let's go to the dressmaker first please."

Three stores and four heavy bags later, Hestia asked,"Why don't the mortals have one convenient place to get all your shopping done?"

"They are too weak minded for such a feat of greatness," Aphrodite answered simply.

"Well, why don't we make this, " Hesita paused to think for a moment "this, um, shopping center?"

"I LOVE THIS IDEA!" Aphrodite exclaimed .

"Let's do it!" Hesita said excited as well.

"Ok, chauffeur take us down to that field". Aphrodite

jumped gracefully out of the chariot to the ground and bumped right into -- "how dare you, a puny mortal, bump into me, the most beautiful of the 12 Olympians," Aphrodite ranted.

"Aphrodite! It's just Artemis," Hestia said walking up to them.

"Hey, good to see you too. Why are you two hanging out?" Artemis asked surprised to see the pair of them.

"Aphrodite took me shopping for a new dress" Hestia said, pointing to chariot overflowing with bags "How is the hunt going these days?"

"Good , good my hunters are searching the perimeters,as we speak, for the Spiked Molean. We suspect its lair is around here somewhere."

"If you must know, you're just in time to witness a great feat of practicality," Aphrodite boasted.

"What?" Artemis said confused.

"Just wait and watch" Hestia said happily, "Do the thing" she said, egging on Aphrodite.

Aphrodite went to the middle of the field and assumed her truest form by raising her arms and levitating while spinning around. As Aphrodite glowed brightly, all her favorite shops and stores came zooming together from all over the world. She gently landed on the ground.

"Voilá! An all practical, Shopping Center."

"Wow" Hestia and Artemis said excitedly.

"It's so practical," Hestia said.

"Go ahead inside," Aphrodite encouraged.

A moment later, the ground began to shake, grumble,and rumble.

"What is happening to my beautiful shopping center ?" Aphrodite screamed.

"It's an earthquake!" Hestia screamed.

"Oh no, It's here!" Artemis yelled to her hunters. As they emerged from the surrounding forest to help protect the Practical Shopping Center. A spiked Molean, it's massive claws, great for digging, came crawling out of the ground.

"Oh! That's how he got away so fast," Artemis said.

"You know this monster?" Hestia shouted over the rumbling as she pulled her flaming sword.

"Yes!" Artemis shouted back. Lieutenant." she yelled as one of her best hunters came running forward, ducking and rolling as she tried to avoid the scratching claws

"My ladies, "the Lieutenant said, kneeling.

"Report," Artemis said.

"The beast has a big weaknesses, but watch for its fangs and claws, that are good for scratching, digging and getting in the way, as we now know. It's very sensitive to light and sound," she said standing up.

"Thank you lieutenant, go rally our hunters," Aetrmis

said, dismissing her lieutenant. All this time, Aphrodite had been silently listening. She spoke just as the Molean fully emerged from the ground, almost destroying the front half of the shopping center. Finally,the ground stopped shaking.

"There is no need for violence," Aphrodite said coolly..

"What!?" both Artemis and Hestia said, confusedly.

"Call your hunters back! Leave it to me!" Aphrodite said confidently.

Artemis did as she was told and Hestia put away her sword. Aphrodite walked out in front of the huge beast and began singing a very beautiful yet melancholy song which brought them all to tears. The force of the song pushed the beast backward, straight into the shopping center's center. Then, she hit the highest note possible, which obliterated the beast's hearing capability. Aretmis ran up and shot an arrow, made from solid moonlight. Being the first huntress she never missed.

"Right on target," she whispered.

It struck the stunned beast right in the heart, turning the beast into stone. The battle was over before it started nearly destroying the Practical Shopping Center. Aphrodite sank to her knees and shed one godly tear. Hestia went to work creating a big hearth to surround the beast where it stood. Artemis caught on fast and started to help Hestia. Two moments later all they needed was Aphrodite to repair the building.....which she did with delight.

"Hunters, QUICKLY shield your eyes, for no mortal shall look upon a goddess's truest form." Artemis said with urgency in her voice.

The Practical Shopping Center was better than before because it had a mystical, petrified beast in the center. Aphrodite let Artemis's hunters be the first mortals to look upon the shopping center as thanks for their protection in its time of need.

The end.

SECTION 4 – IT'S ABOUT LOVE

The Hidden Colors of Mrs. John Holton

By Kate Voltz (2020 Second Place)

You wake up to white sheets, white even in the darkness of your unlit bedroom. Your husband is still asleep beside you, but you have to get up before he does.

Turn off the alarm. Rub your eyes and get up. Shower. Scrub off the little marks you didn't catch yesterday, the flecks of color against your hands that could serve as evidence of your sole secret. Get dressed, powder your face. Listen as your children stumble down the stairs. Say a cheery 'good morning!' and smile. Turn on the coffee and the stovetop. Tap perfectly white eggs against the pan, watch the yolks spill out. Pour your husband coffee into your nice, unchipped ceramic mugs. Smile. Serve breakfast. Smile.

Don't start thinking about the what-if, if-only, I-wishes. Those aren't meant for downstairs.

Make a remark about the weather, or maybe the news if it's not political. Give your kids and husband their lunches.

Smile, and close the door. Sigh.

They're gone now. The exhaust from your husband's car is melting into the cold January air, and your children's footsteps are the only marks in the otherwise unmarred snow. Inside, the clock is ticking, slowly and surely, echoing around the creamy walls of the downstairs. The kitchen, with its shiny alabaster tiles, is colder than the living room. Pacing now, you walk around the downstairs, over the carpet and to the hardwood stairs, which click under your embroidered slippers. Your dry hands and magenta fingernails skim the white rail and tan wall on either side of you as you ascend. Against those creamy colors, your painted nails seem garish and dark. As you reach the top of the stairs, you look up and reach. A single, thin and entirely bleached nylon rope dangles lightly in the air, and you pull it, unleashing a cascade of creaking silver metal - the stairs to the attic. The steel is tarnished and chipped, and so is the silver pull chain for the ceiling lamp in the attic.

All around the attic, in every direction, are sprawling white towers of covering clothes. A few have a few specks of color, a few anonymous splatters, but mostly they are pearly white and everywhere. In the center of the room, an easel sits. Waiting. The stacks of white in the attic are reminiscent of beehives, you think. Beehives, maybe in a meadow, maybe in a field with violet and rosy wildflowers, where the oak trees cast mottled shadows against the waving grasses and where the bees can dance and buzz quietly and to themselves, and where the air doesn't smell of cologne and scrambled eggs. You approach the canvas on the easel and begin. And though you can't feel your fingers in the cold attic air, you feel the warm and gentle breeze on your arms and in your hair.

You're there, if only for a brief and entirely luminous moment. You are there.

That night, making dinner, there are little dots of color on your pale hand, on your fingers, on your silver wedding ring. In the shower, the ring chafes against your skin as you rub to expunge the small dot of green. That night, in your papery white sheets, on your magenta nails, there's another color: a gentle cerulean blue. You scrape it off with another finger, leaving a crescent indentation in the polish.

"I can't believe this. I really can't," said Alice, pacing the walls of the gallery. Brightly colored paintings scattered the walls. One of a hydrangea, blooming at the top but withered at the bottom. One of a lighthouse overlooking a sea with an incoming storm. "How could we not know? There are hundreds of these. And they're incredible, that art critic just said so," she said.

Her brother replied, "I know. It's just... I don't know, Alice." A pause. The white walls of the gallery were blinding, glaringly white. The only reprieve was to stare fixedly at the paintings, which was what most of the buyers were doing anyways. "Do you think she was happy?"

"I don't know," said Alice quietly. "And now they're both gone." Another pause. Alice sighed. "Maybe we'll never know." They both stared at the paintings. In the fluorescent indoor lighting, all of the paintings seemed to be defiant, refusing to be white against the paint of the walls and the dark grey tile floor. Alice stared at the floor instead.

Elizabeth Holton, 1938-2020: Holton (née Laustet) was known for her realism and scenery, as well as her unique use of color and brushstroke patterns to convey emotion. Her works were only discovered by her family after her death; they were sold posthumously by her children, shocking the art world with more than 600 paintings of astonishing quality. Her intricacy, detail, and worldly yet mundane subjects have ensured her place as one of the most impactful painters of this century.

*Author's note: this story is fiction. Any similarities to real-life people or events are purely coincidental.

Do You Believe in Love at First Sight?

By Blake Willett (Finalist)

One day, as I sat watching the television with my granddaughter, she turned and asked with youthful idealism, "Granny, do you believe in love at first sight?"

I took a moment to gather myself. "Well…"

When I was young, it was the age of booze and good times, and everyone got careless about consequences. It was one particularly careless night that started it all.

"It'll only be a small gathering," Mindy had said. As I stared at the milling field of crisp suits and drop-waist dresses, I realized just how much of an understatement that was. The boys, cheated out of the War by being born a few years too late, wore bomber jackets and cocky grins that only showed off their naivety. We girls danced round like flower stalks in the breeze. I, too, swung from partner to partner in a swirl of color and laughter.

As I tumbled into one of my classmates, I saw him.

He leaned against a tree with quiet confidence. He stood all alone but didn't look lonely as he watched the dancers. My stubborn self saw no reason for him to be left out of the fun, so I asked him to dance with me.

"I don't dance. Plenty of fun to watch." He nodded a farewell with a wave from his glass. Alas, he had no idea who he was dealing with.

As he turned away, I grabbed his arm and tugged him towards the mass of dancing bodies. "Everyone dances. It expresses joy, and, oh, what a day to be alive!" I exclaimed. He hesitantly gave in, and we were soon swaying a smooth waltz near the edge of the crowd.

As we danced, we conversed, and I learned about a calm, reserved boy named James. He listened to me, too, quietly and without judgment. It was peaceful, to just be with someone else, among the crush of activity. We soon slipped into a comfortable silence as the party slowly dissolved around us.

Regretfully, I looked up at him. "I'm already past curfew. I have to go now." I slowly disentangled our fingers and limbs.

He grabbed my arm, and asked in a hushed whisper, "Would you like me to come see you again, Miss Morelli?"

Turning away to hide the flames in my cheeks I briskly called over my shoulder, "Call me Adelina next time."

I didn't look back, but, boy, was I tempted.

My heels clicked down the empty sidewalk, echoing

down the alleys and up the brick apartment buildings. My building came up and, persuaded by the heavy hesitance in the air, I looked up at the faraway moon before ascending the creaking stairwell.

As I pushed open the door, my ma swung out of the kitchen in a billow of fabric. "Hi, darling," she trilled, cheeks flushed. "Look at you, my pretty girl!" She tugged on my dress. "Look at you, so on top of those new fashions. But, oh, I can't tease you. Maybe you'll impress some rich capitalist. Then we can finally get out of this slum, away... away from all this..."

She looked as if she could see something I couldn't, something so heartbreaking, she couldn't tear her eyes away. A tear rolled slowly down the hollows of her cheek and fell into her trembling mouth. She swayed, shuddered, then collapsed into my arms, and I could smell the alcohol on her breath.

"I'm sorry. I'm so sorry I can't provide more for you. You know I love you, that you are my treasure, that you are beautiful and loved. You know that, right? I am so sorry your stupid mother can't do more to support you. I am so sorry!" She went on like that for a while before she finally quieted and I led her gently to her bed.

The following weeks with James were a blur of smiles among my melancholy surroundings. He was never boring and I soon discovered, by way of the extravagant places he took me, that he was quite wealthy. I enjoyed our bantering conversations, which always ended with his quiet, humorous smile, and I thought this bliss could really last forever.

The sun was fading over the horizon and we meandered down the lane towards my house. It would have been romantic, walking in the warm light of sunset, had it not been for the nervous way he kept twitching his hand in mine. He finally turned to me with a sigh.

"This has been fun, and you are so sweet…"

"Oh, you give me too much credit. You're the one who took me out for a lobster dinner." I smiled at him and tugged his hand to pull him closer. He stumbled forward and fell silent.

"It has been fun, but we both know this just wasn't going to last, right? I'm going away to university next week, and I think we should stop seeing each other. I mean, look at yourself. Look at your house." He looked at me expectantly, but all I could do was stand in shock. "Lina?"

I turned and ran inside.

I remember my momma once told me to never cry over a boy, because if he made me cry he wasn't worth it. I tried. I really did. But as I shut the door behind me, the dam came crashing down, and all I remember after that was the flood of tears and hopelessness.

I sighed as I turned to my grandbaby. "To answer your question, no. I don't believe in love at first sight. But it works out alright in the end. He might not be the one, but there will be someone who makes you happy."

There was a rustle from the kitchen and a slow-moving man emerged. "What would you like for dinner, love?" His gentle hand came to rest on my shoulder. Overwhelmed with happiness, I could only look at my husband with blurry eyes.

Yes. It all works out alright.

Forever

By Alyssa Noseworthy (Finalist and Honorable Mention)

Noah always felt his age in his bones; his back ached more and more, and the arthritis flared up almost daily. He also felt it in his ears: he knew that the sounds around him would have once been deafening, but now, they were quiet, barely audible from decades of hearing loss. Still, he knew what the sounds were, as much as he wished he did not.

How many people would be wounded, injured...even killed...in the name of living forever? It was a question that had festered in him like an infection, plaguing him ever since he had first seen the signposts of rebellion.

He wondered how the government had been so blind to something obvious to a man with worsening cataracts. How had they not seen the banners, caught like sails in the wind, proclaiming "Bourgeoisie! Bourgeoisie! Bourgeoisie!" How had they not seen the discontent in the faces of the very same people who had funded this project, who had poured their income into it through taxes and donations?

It stood now, gleaming in little glass vials before him, vats of purple liquid. He wondered how something so small and insignificant could have ruined a country—a world—so quickly. Each vial could not have been bigger than his thumb.

His granddaughter had begged and pleaded with him not to go. She, too, had been fooled, thinking he was some revolutionary in the midst of trying to reclaim what was rightfully his. It was better that she thought that, in retrospect. If she had really known, she would have dismissed him as insane long before he would have ever managed to attend one of the club's meetings.

He had no illusions about this little vial belonging to him. In truth, the right to immortality belonged to no one. He had not come to claim it; he had come to destroy it.

He thought, sometimes, that if immortality could make his granddaughter's smile last forever, it might just be worth everything it had claimed to be. But even then, he knew that was selfishness. Humanity had fixated on whether it was possible, and not whether it was moral. When people had forgotten what they should do, in being mystified by the potential of what they could do...that was when everything had started unraveling.

It had all started when the product was initially released. It had been distributed at exorbitant prices, only possibly affordable to the ultra-rich. Scientists cited that it was necessary—not only was it expensive to make, but if immortality was distributed to everyone, population control issues would arise and the environmental impact of such a move would be detrimental. How the lower and middle classes, even the upper income gradients which stood on the cusp of being able to afford it...how they had all united, these disparate people, in the common goal of hating those who had done this to them...

Of all things, immortality should not be marketed. It wasn't supposed to be plastered in advertisements, packaged and offered in commercials. What hubris! What arrogance, conceit, and egoism had ruled the creation of such a monstrosity!

When the revolutionaries had broken through the gate, they might as well have stormed the Bastille. They had come in a great wave, like a flood destined to wipe out all of humanity. Forces had been sent to "keep the peace," although the objective seemed laughable to him, if not for the fact that the irony tasted so bitter. He had never understood how weapons could be used to maintain "peace."

Now, as the revolutionaries surged, crashed against these forces, like an ocean clattering, colliding against rocks, now, as the fighting raged rampantly like an inferno...

He had waded through the labyrinth of halls, to where they had speculated the serum was kept. It had been a maze of corridors steeped with shadows, obscure and murky in the dimness. Each passageway had looked identical to the next, branching forward in a haphazard tangle. Even now, he felt that finally arriving to this room had almost been an accident, a coincidence, or perhaps call it fate...

He heard footsteps approaching. The loud, heavy tread of military boots, not revolutionaries. Regardless, no one coming would have been sympathetic to him. Now was the only time he had.

He raised his arms above his head, ignoring the twinge of his arthritis as he did so.

"Turn around!" A gruff voice screamed.

He realized that his arms, the way they were, probably looked like a sign of surrender.

They were to be his greatest gesture of defiance.

He thought of his granddaughter, how beautiful she looked with ribbons in her hair…

He thought of the beauty of a mortal, finite life. He thought that he had lived long enough. He thought that the gray of his hair, the wrinkles of his face, and the wood of his walking-stick were all far more valuable than a thousand wasted lifetimes.

Martyr…was that what he would be? Is that what history would remember him as? Hero, villain, radical?

"I said, turn around!"

His ears barely even registered the sound. It was just another quiet, almost silent, barrage of noise that hearing loss had muted for him.

To a better world, he thought.

He brought his arms down, and the vials shattered.

You Don't Have to Understand

By Ariana Dyer (Finalist)

A little girl walked through the streets of her city. Her coat was red, bright and bloody against the ashen backdrop. Behind her, a mother, emerging from a bomb shelter. In her arms the woman carried an infant, swaddled in dusty, gray rags. Pushing the young girl aside, the woman stumbled down the street with the silent baby, off to see if her home was still standing. The girl walked slowly through the broken street, unfazed by the bodies that were scattered, smudged around the edges by the white haze that had painted the air the night before. She had not been welcomed into the safety of a bunker, and her dark hair was dusted with ash. As she walked, buildings loomed out from the whiteness of the morning. Screams pierced the scene, muffled by the smoke. Soon, her soft footsteps began to echo off of the walls of an alley, the sound dulled by the thick air and the ringing in her ears. She approached a small nest made of old blankets covered in a once-bright silk tarp and crawled into the small space. Lying on the soft, worn fabric of someone's old winter coat, her brown eyes fixed on the corner of the silk, the edge of a design. A white star sitting in a backdrop of blue, red lines smeared beneath it. The girl had seen this design in school long ago, but she didn't have it in her to wonder. She focused instead on the welcoming stillness of the air, and the dusty smell of old clothing.

A noise came from the end of the alley. The girl turned her head, struggling to make out a silhouette walking towards her. She snatched the stick from the opening of her enclosure, allowing the silk cloth to fall over her; fear settled itself on her skin. Her father's words echoed in her ears, and she shivered.

She peeked out from underneath the cloth at the strange man who stood before her and marveled at him, at the sight of him. His hair, bright orange in the darkness of the alley, was tied back into an unruly bundle that stretched past his waist. On his wiry frame hung a black suit with long tails that nearly touched the ground. In the dusty, white air, the man almost seemed to glow.

She watched him bend over the body of a kitten, still and lifeless in the dust. She had noticed the tiny thing as she was walking down the alley, had seen that it was dead. Raising the silk a little higher above her curious eyes, she wondered what he could want with such an animal.

In his hands, the cat stretched. She heard it yawn, saw it shake the fine white dust from its fur. It rubbed against the man's leg, but left no mark on the fabric. She hardly had time to notice the strangeness of the clean, black clothes before the cat was pulling at the silk of her shelter. The tarp that she clung to began to slip away. A baby's cry wound eerily through the streets and into the alley, but the girl heard nothing but the pounding of her heart in her ears as she prepared herself for what would come when she was revealed.

"You can come out, child." She started at the sound of the man's voice. Slowly, she rose from her nest and stepped towards the stranger. "It is nice to see you."

"It's nice to meet you too, sir." She wondered why he looked so familiar to her. She was afraid, but remembered that her father had taught her to always be polite to the strangers that might approach her. "Do you know my father?"

The man looked her over for a long time. "Yes, I know him."

"Have you seen him?"

His gaze was steady on her, unpolluted by the fear that had always plagued and wrinkled the faces of her neighbors. "I've seen him, but he's going to be gone for a little while longer."

The girl studied him suspiciously. "You don't look German."

"I'm not German, but I'm not anything else either."

"How did you fix the cat?"

The man thought for a long time. "Life is very fragile, it can end quickly, like..." the man struggled to find the word, "a sentence. A long time ago, I learned how to put all of the words back in the right order."

"Are you a doctor?"

"No, Mila. Not a doctor."

The child thought for a moment. "How do you know my

name? Did my father tell you?"

The man listened to the sound of airplane engines high above them. Mila did not notice. "Your father wanted me to make sure that you went to the right place when the time came. Soon you'll see him again."

"My father told me to run if anyone tried to take me to him." The girl took a step towards the end of the alley.

"I'm just here as a favor to him, Mila. I'm going to show you how to get home."

"My home is gone."

The sound of airplane engines was loud now, weighing heavily on the air above the city, bathing it in the promise of panic and death.

"There's a new home waiting for you."

The girl looked frantically to the sky.

"I don't understand."

The man held his hand out to her. The dust that had settled into his hair and on his jacket fell to the ground, and he was again spotless.

The air shivered in anticipation as the ground began to shake with explosions. The young girl found herself clinging to the man's coat, the black threads glowing brighter beneath her fingers.

"Mister, you have to run!"

He smiled at her, and placed one gentle hand on her head. The dust lifted from her body. "Not anymore, Mila. Your father is waiting for us."

Watch Out

By Leanne Abel (Finalist)

The last thing I remember was watching the oversize-load truck barreling down the street and me screaming,

"Watch Out!" Everything went black after that.

I open my eyes just a sliver to see where I am. There are doctors, nurses, one of those machines that are used in movies that beeps and tells you whether you're still alive or not. My mom is standing next to my dad, who is wearing a hospital gown. They are both crying. I open my eyes all the way and my parents come over and start crying even more—but I think those are happy tears. I am very confused. What happened? I open my mouth to ask them, but I can't breathe in enough to speak. I only have enough room in my lungs to breathe, and then, just barely. I am very concerned. Why can't I talk? A doctor comes over.

"Cayla, when the truck hit your dad's car, your lung got impaled by a sharp object. You got a surgery to seal up the hole, but you still can't breathe on your own." He points to a machine to my right that must be the thing saving my life. "You don't have enough strength back to talk, either. You'll have two more surgeries to get you speaking and breathing normally again." He smiles and walks away. When the truck hit my dad's car? Did we get into an accident with the truck? It makes sense: my dad and I both in hospital gowns. I look over to the doctor talking with my parents and I overhear part of their conversation.

"...she'll never be able to participate in gym anymore. It uses too much breathing. No running, swimming, biking, or climbing mountains... Does she do any other activities?" My parents look at each other and nod.

"She plays the trombone," my mom tells the doctor, who shakes his head.

"She won't be able to do that anymore." I can't play the trombone anymore? Band is my favorite period in the day. The reason I am in marching band and a part of who I am. I can't just give that up because my lungs stopped working. A tear slides down my check, but I can't let all the crying out because that "wouldn't be allowed." I don't know if I would be able to do it either. I am so scared right now. My lungs aren't working correctly and I don't know how I should breathe. A couple nurses come over and ask me if I'm okay. I can't talk, but if I could, I don't think I would have said anything. The doctor and my parents come over and start all asking if I'm okay. All the commotion makes me dizzier than I was before and I blank out again.

"Cayla, honey?" My mother is shaking me awake and I groggily open my eyes. "The doctor needs to give you something to make you stay asleep during the surgeries." I nod and the doctor hands me something in a cup. I drink it and immediately fall back asleep.

I open my eyes without anyone waking me up. I am in the same room as I was the first time I woke up in this hospital. I've been awake for such a short amount of time that I almost forget why I'm here. Almost. My mom comes over.

"We can leave now, sweetie. Dad had to go home to take care of your brother." I nod and stand up, but almost fall over. My mom steadies me and we walk out of the hospital together. When we get in the car and are driving along the highway, my mom leans over to me.

"You know you can talk again." I look over at her, my eyes widened. I smile.

"Really?" I am shocked by the sound of my own voice, the same one I've heard so many times and thought nothing of. You really don't know what you've lost until it's gone.

Nick, my little brother, comes up to me as I walk through the front door. He pulls on my arm.

"Are you okay?" I smile at his adorable worried face.

"Nick, Cayla needs to go to sleep. She's had a rough couple days." I nod and walk upstairs to my room and slip on my own pajamas. No hospital gown anymore. Going to sleep has never been easier.

I walk into school the next day and people keep coming up to me and asking where I've been and how I'm doing. I appreciate their concern, but I wish everyone wasn't talking to me. But, as annoying as it is, I would rather talk to everyone in the entire school than go to band. Sit in my first chair spot and not be able to play along with my section. I know I'm not supposed to, but I hold my breath for a second. I wait a couple minutes and do it again. Second period is Spanish. I hold my breath for two seconds. A couple minutes later, I do it again. Third period, three seconds. Fourth period, four seconds. Five and five. Six and six. Seven and seven. Eight and eight. Nine and nine. On the bus, I can hold my breath for ten seconds. The doctor said I wouldn't be able to hold my breath for more than one second. By holding it over and over again, I can do ten.

When I get home, I go to my room and take out my trombone. As quietly as possible, I start playing scales. I have to take a breath in the middle on the way up and down. I switch to my music. I can play one measure in one breath. One and a half. Two. Two and a half. Three. Three and a half. Four. My mom knocks on my door. I get scared when she opens it, but she is smiling.

"Cayla Blakely: miracle worker. Watch out."

Sunflowers

By Alyssa Smith (Finalist)

Bright and strong
Our yellow faces create a sea of
Liquid gold
Bending and rippling in the breeze
Beauty in the many and the few
We honor the sun with upturned eyes and
Love-filled hearts
Our soft, velvety bodies standing tall and proud
 "She loves me,
She loves me not"
Symbol of happiness and love
Shining
Night comes and we bow our heads
Waiting
Until dawn

Riverdale Bridge

By Cody Bowen (Finalist)

January 12th - 9:00 pm

"Stop suicide, Make a difference!" yelled Wendy, as she held up a sign. She stopped yelling and put her sign down. She reached down and pulled a water bottle out of her bag. She took the cap off and took a drink. She set the drink down and put on her beenie. She rubbed her hands together to keep warm. It was at least 30 degrees outside and it was starting to snow. A woman walked up to Wendy and read her sign aloud. "Share a hug. Not suicide." She looked back up at Wendy and hugged her. "Thank you, I needed that. Life is hard right now," said the woman, while patting Wendy's back. "I'll be here for you." Wendy said with a smile. The woman shared a smile and she walked away. Wendy turned around to get another drink of water and she looked over to see a boy wearing a hood, looking over the bridge. She picked up her sign and walked towards him. She put the sign up in front of him. He looked at it and then at her. He wiped a tear off of his face. She put the sign down and hugged him. He started crying.

"Shhhh, it's okay. I am here for you," Wendy said.

She picked up her sign and walked back over to her bag. She reached down and took a swig of her water. She put it back down and picked her sign back up so the approaching man could read it. "Stop suicide, share a hug." A tall man walked up to her and read her sign.

"You really think you can make a difference? Just because you sit out here with a sign. Don't mean your gonna save anyone. Do you do this for a reason?"

Wendy looked up at him with tears in her eyes. "Yes sir. I do this for a reason," she said. "Then why do you do it?" the tall man asked. "My son. He was bullied. He didn't think there was any way out. He told me one afternoon he was gonna go for a drive to clear his mind, and that he would be home later.

But He never came home. He drove his truck off of this bridge. Right here, where I stand. And he died on impact. So I stand here to stop somebody from doing what my son did. To help someone." The man looked at her sadly. "Dang lady, I'm sorry, but you standing here is not gonna make a difference. Suicides happen every day. You can't stop it." Wendy looked up at him and wiped her tears off of her face and smiled, "Well, I'll try my best." she said. That's when she heard a woman screaming and running. She ran up to the boy wearing the hood, looking over the bridge, He turned around. With tears in his eyes and hugged the woman. The two shared a conversation and he looked over at Wendy and pointed at her and smiled. Wendy looked at them and smiled and waved. The woman grabbed the boy by the hand and walked over to Wendy. "Oh my gosh, thank you!" screamed the woman, while hugging Wendy.

"May I ask what I have done?" Asked Wendy.

"You saved my son. He was going to commit suicide. I came home from work and found this letter on my counter." she reached in her purse and pulled out a letter. The tall man looked at the letter and then at Wendy. He cracked a smile and shook his head, "Well, I stand corrected. It's true that one person can make a difference." Wendy smiled and looked back at the mother and son.

"Well I'm glad to help you." Wendy said, shedding a tear. She wiped her tears out of her eyes. The mother hugged Wendy again "God bless you. Thank you so much." You can make a difference. Suicide isn't a joke, help someone out in your community.

With Wings as Eagles

By Breanna Cothran (Finalist)

It had all led up to this. Anxiety induced nightmares where I couldn't stay in between the lines or my muscles solidified into unyielding marble had forced me to learn to plough through fear. Shooting pains, dull aches, and rigid knots had forced me to persevere in spite of discomfort. Hours spent running down this goal, stretching and straining for every second, I would spend to buy less than thirty seconds per go in this stadium. I jogged onto the track to compete for the first time, trying to pretend like I was unbothered by the intimidating muscle development of the girls surrounding me. My teammates behind me reassured me that I knew what I was doing and I was entirely capable of performing what needed to be done. Time moved unhurriedly forward while I suppressed my terror and panic.

I walked to my spot as the second leg and waited. My hands began to tingle, my rib cage constricted around my organs, I began to feel lightheaded and my eyes burned with unshed tears. The anticipation was steadily building as I stared

149

down the daunting red ring of rubber and glanced around at the confident faces of our adversaries. Soon every leg was ready. Our first leg was prepared at the starting line set in her blocks, and my trepidation reached a deafening crescendo in my head before the sharp crack of the gun quelled it with a swift blanket of acceptance.

The girls launched out of their blocks and propelled forward with every stride, exerting their dominance over the track. All of them faded away except for the one running for me, and I waited with nothing in my mind and tense legs as she approached. When she was about a yard and a half away from me, I burst forward and listened for her to call out. "Stick!", she shouted, and I threw my arm back to receive the baton. My time had arrived, and I could make it or break it, as could any one of us. With the baton secure in my fingertips, I accelerated and focused solely on passing the girl to the right of me. She was about a car's length away. There was no time to be tired and no time to lose focus. It was only me and her and the distance that was growing shorter exhale by gruff exhale. In what seemed like less than ten seconds, I was nearly handing it off to my teammate and had advanced to two steps behind the girl in the lane outside of ours. The moment I yelled "Stick!", I moved a step ahead of her. Then the stick was passed on and my job was done. It was time to watch and wait; Although, I wished I had been able to run about twenty more meters so that I could have put more distance between us.

Our third leg passed it off to our fourth, and she flew. I knew we had it the moment she rocketed forward. We waited by the platforms and I reassured our anchor that we had secured it, and we did. We won first place at the state track meet of 2018 by a tenth of a second, and I recalled the bible verse our coach had recited to us as encouragement while they placed the gold medals around our necks. "But they that wait upon the Lord shall renew their strength; they shall mount up with wings as eagles; they shall run, and not be weary; and they shall walk, and not faint" (Isaiah 40:31, King James Version). Supposedly he had flipped to it randomly. I was not very religious, but that verse would stick with me, and even though the medal around my neck was not genuine gold, it might as well have been.

Cool Imagination Titles

Convergence by Brian Claspell
Jim Conrad may not be as fictional as the CIA thinks. Pick up *Convergence*, a mystery-thriller, on Amazon and at other fine retailers.

One Spark *- Short Story Anthology 2011-2018*
Enjoy reading the short stories of all the winners (2011-2018) and 2018 finalist of the "Imagination Begins with You..." high school writing contest. All proceeds support scholarships.

One Spark *– "Imagination Begins with You..." 2019*
Jump into reading finalist stories from the "Imagination Begins with You..." high school writing contest. All proceeds support scholarships.

One Spark *– "Imagination Begins with You..." 2020*
"Imagination Begins with You..." high school writing contest is an annual writing contest open. The finalist and winners are published in an annual short story collection where all proceeds support scholarships. Enjoy!